A
Harlequin
Romance

WELCOME

TO THE WONDERFUL WORLD

of Harlequin Romances!

Interesting, informative and entertaining,
each Harlequin Romance portrays an appealing
love story. Harlequin Romances take you
to faraway places — places with real people
facing real love situations — and
you become part of their story.

As publishers of Harlequin Romances, we're extremely
proud of our books (we've been publishing
them since 1954). We're proud also that Harlequin
Romances are North America's most-read
paperback romances.

Eight new titles are released every month and are
sold at nearly all book-selling stores across
Canada and the United States.

A free catalogue listing all available Harlequin Romances
can be yours by writing to the

HARLEQUIN READER SERVICE,
M.P.O. Box 707, Niagara Falls, N.Y. 14302.
Canadian address: Stratford, Ontario, Canada.

or use order coupon at back of book.

We sincerely hope you enjoy reading
this Harlequin Romance.

Yours truly,

THE PUBLISHERS
   Harlequin Romances

MOONLIGHT AND MAGIC

by

RACHEL LINDSAY

HARLEQUIN BOOKS   TORONTO
WINNIPEG

Original hard cover edition published in 1962
by Mills & Boon Limited, 17-19 Foley Street,
London W1A 1DR, England

© Scribe Associates Ltd. 1962

Harlequin edition published December 1972

SBN 373-01648-4

Printed in Canada

CHAPTER ONE

JANE BERRY switched the telephone from one ear to the other and ran a hand through her blonde hair. 'Honestly,' she groaned, 'you'd think I was trying to speak to the Dalai Lama!'

Maggie Simpson glanced up from her typewriter. 'Give it up,' she advised. 'Dinky Howard's got no time for the press.'

'Except when he needs us. If I—' Jane broke off as a voice sounded in her ear. 'Mr. Howard, this is Jane Berry of the *Morning Star*. I wonder if I could see you for a few minutes? Our readers are interested in the cruise you're organizing and ... But, Mr. Howard, the *Star* would never—'

Her words were cut short by a sharp click at the other end, and with a grimace she banged down the receiver.

Maggie laughed. 'And another scoop bites the dust! You should know the great Mr. Howard never gives interviews.'

'That's just what he told me – only less politely. "Tell your editor my friends have no wish to see their names in his scandal sheet!"' Angrily Jane picked up a sheet of paper. 'Just look at the passenger list. Lord and Lady Waterton, the Duchess of Melford, David Pickton...' Her eye travelled down the names. 'Film stars, racehorse owners, driving aces – it's a gossip columnist's dream.'

'And a matchmaker's paradise,' Maggie retorted. 'Any millionaire who goes on one of Dinky's cruises can be certain of one thing – no girl he meets there will be after his money, because she'll already be loaded!'

Jane sighed. 'What wouldn't I give for a chance to go on a cruise like that!'

'Since when were you a gold-digger?'

'I was talking as a reporter,' Jane said indignantly.

'A naïve one, then. When you've met as many million-aires as I have you'll find them as dull as the boy next door – and considerably older!' Maggie skimmed through her type-script with a practised eye and then she looked up. 'Stop acting ruffled, Berry, I was only kidding you. You're lucky if you *can* remain naïve in this business. Most of us get too hard-boiled.' She clipped her pages together and rang for the copy boy.

Jane watched, envying her efficiency. The older girl was every inch a newspaperwoman and a match for any male reporter on the Street. The copy boy came in for the type-script, and Maggie groped in a drawer of her desk and brought out soap and towel.

'Thank goodness I've finished on time. I'm going to a show and I daren't be late.'

She was half-way across the room when the door opened and Frank Preston, the Features Editor, came in. He looked at the towel in Maggie's hand and nodded. 'That's right, freshen yourself up. You're going to a party.'

'On the contrary. Bill's taking me to a show.'

'Bill *was* taking you. Sorry, Maggie, but Charlie's just phoned in. He's tied up at London Airport and can't make tonight's shindig at the Saville. Positively last appearance of Ruby Randall before retirement. We daren't miss it.'

Maggie's face puckered with annoyance. 'This'll make the third time I've stood Bill up this week!'

'He should know better than to date a newspaperwoman!' Frank shrugged. 'Take him with you, no one will object.'

'Except Bill. He loathes that sort of party.'

'Too bad! As a sociologist he should appreciate the op-portunity for research.'

'You're a callous brute, Frank.'

'This is a newspaper we work for, not a monthly glossy!'

Jane watched the by-play in front of her, her amusement dissolving as she noticed Maggie's hands clenched at her sides.

'Couldn't I go instead?' she asked.

The Features Editor stared at her, and as she saw his doubt, Jane's stubborn streak came to the fore. 'It won't be the first reception I've covered,' she insisted.

He hesitated. 'How long have you been on the column?'

'Six months. And before that I was a year in the news room. I covered dozens of parties while I was there.'

'There's more to this one than meets the eye. We don't give a hoot for Ruby's retirement; what we're looking for are the undercurrents behind it.'

'If you give me the briefing,' Jane said more confidently than she felt, 'I'm sure I can do it.'

'Okay then. Come and see me in five minutes and I'll have the files down for you to run through. As for you, Maggie, my advice is marry the guy. That way he'll *have* to stand for it.'

He took himself off and Maggie squeezed Jane's shoulder.

'If ever I take Frank's advice, you must be bridesmaid,' she said.

The Saville Hotel was near the *Morning Star* offices, and Jane, fresh from her briefing, decided to walk. Despite her outward air of confidence, eighteen months as a reporter had not quelled the nervous tingling at the base of her spine before each new assignment, and she was anxious to get the coming job formulated in her mind.

'No interviews,' the Features Editor counselled. 'Just sniff around for general atmosphere. And if you get taken for a guest, so much the better.'

This last was not difficult. With Maggie's type as most people's idea of a woman reporter, Jane's appearance made her profession difficult to guess – model, film star or working débutante being the three most likely occupations attributed to her. Delicate features added to the illusion of fragility, though a perceptive observer would have recognized stubbornness in the heart-shaped face and determination in the short straight nose and sensitive mouth. But most observers, being far from perceptive, saw only the pale skin and honey-gold hair and the unexpected beauty of vivid blue eyes.

The hall porter in the lobby of the Saville Hotel was no exception to this general reaction as he checked her press invitation.

'Reporter, are you, miss? Took you for one of the star-lets!'

Jane smiled and walked into the Embassy Room where the reception was being held. Edging her way towards the bar, she was able to identify a number of faces. The 'fringe element', as they were known in the features room of the *Morning Star*, were to be seen at every social function, continually striving to catch the eye of the gossip columnists and find their name bracketed with the famous in the next day's editions.

Strategically positioned against a corner of the bar with a drink in her hand, Jane eavesdropped shamelessly as the tide of gossip eddied around her. Across the room she caught a glimpse of the tightly corseted figure of Ruby Randall, long time leading lady of musical comedy but now better known for her marital adventures. Her latest boy-friend was no-where to be seen, but cigar-chewing Foster Dillon, director of Ace Films and number three in Ruby's hierarchy of hus-bands, was everywhere in evidence. Jane began mentally to compose her story.

'For heaven's sake, Glyn,' a girl's voice said behind her, 'if you can't hold your drink like a man, stick to ginger beer.'

Simultaneously there was a hiccough in Jane's ear and the young man in question lurched against her, sending the con-tents of her glass splashing down her dress.

'I say, old girl, can't – hic – tell you how – hic – sorry I am.' His face puckered with distress, and ineffectually he began to dab Jane's skirt with his handkerchief.

'Can't you see you're making it worse?' The girl beside him, a pretty blonde in a pink dress, snatched the handkerchief from him, and staring at her Jane felt she had seen her somewhere before. 'I must apologize for Glyn,' the girl continued. 'One drink and he can't see straight!' She touched Jane's arm. 'I'm staying at this hotel, so why not come up to my room and I'll lend you something to change into.'

Before Jane could reply she found herself being propelled through the crowd towards the exit, and a few moments later was whirring up in the lift to the quietness of the fifth floor. Down to the end of the corridor they went and entered a magnificently furnished bedroom filled with bowls of flowers.

Her reporter's eye took in the sable stole on the bed and the expensive luggage stacked by the wall before her companion flung open the wardrobe door and gestured towards the dresses hanging there.

'Take your pick,' she invited indifferently.

The wardrobe door was mirrored on the inside, and as Jane stepped forward, both girls were reflected in it. Jane caught her breath and the other laughed at her astonishment.

'I wondered how long it would be before you noticed.'

Jane swung round. 'We could be sisters!'

'We could almost be twins.' The girl turned to the dressing-table and with deft fingers pulled her hair into the less sculptured style favoured by Jane. With the golden waves brushing softly against her shoulders, half her sophistication vanished and her resemblance to Jane increased even further. 'There we are; see what I mean?'

'It's uncanny,' Jane said.

'I know, and it's just what I'm looking for.' The girl sat on the bed. 'My name's Janey, incidentally. Janey Belton.'

'I'm Jane too. Jane Berry.'

'Even the name's the same! This is getting positively creepy.' Janey Belton leaned forward; the smile had left her face and there was a sadness in her expression that could not be ignored. 'You seem like an intelligent person. What

9

brought you to that grisly party?'

'I'm a reporter.'

'I see! In that case, I'm sure you've heard of me.'

'Belton?' Jane's mind began to tick over. 'Wait a minute – d'you mean Belton's Bread?'

'Right first time. It's my father!'

Jane whistled softly. There was a Belton's bakery and restaurant in every city and town throughout the country. If this girl was Cedric Belton's daughter she must be heiress to millions. Fleetingly she wondered why a girl with undeniable beauty and money should have such an air of *tristesse*.

Janey swung her feet over the edge of the bed, her voice hard. 'And now you realize who I am, I suppose you're busy envying me?'

'Not at all, Miss Belton. Money is not synonymous with happiness in *my* life.'

'Thank goodness for that. At least it makes it easier for me to talk to you.' She hesitated momentarily. 'When that drink spilled over you downstairs it must have been an act of fate. Until it happened I'd not noticed you, but once I did – and I saw how alike we were – I knew that you were the answer to my prayer. You're the one person who can help me.'

Jane's curiosity was aroused and she moved away from the wardrobe, all thought of putting on a model dress forgotten in the excitement of a possible story. 'If you could begin at the beginning,' she suggested, 'I might be able to follow you. What's it all about?'

'What do you think?' Janey Belton was defiant. 'A man, of course.'

'Oh!' For some reason Jane had not been prepared for the obvious.

'You sound disappointed.' Janey stared down at her hands. 'I'm not surprised, though – it's a pretty banal story. His name is Ted Wills and I love him desperately.'

'Doesn't *he* love *you*?'

'Not according to my father. He says he's only after my money, and Dad's told me that so often I'm even beginning to believe it myself.' She laughed harshly. 'Oh, Ted loves me all right, but Dad thinks he's a fortune-hunter and won't let us get married.'

'How old is Ted?'

'Twenty-six. He's an engineer and he's just opened a garage in Middleford – where we live. Everything he's saved has gone into the garage and he's broke to the wide.' Now that Janey had started to talk, the words came out in a rush. 'We met when I took my car to him after I'd had an accident. I didn't want Dad to know about it, he's always on to me about driving too fast, and if I'd taken it to our usual place he'd have found out.

'Anyway, Ted fixed it up for me and let me pay the bill in instalments. I know I'm an heiress, but Dad never gives me money. He likes to pay everything – it's the only way he can keep control over everyone.'

A picture of Cedric Belton flashed into Jane's mind: he looked exactly the sort of man his daughter had described.

'But what's wrong with Ted?' she asked. 'I mean, you've got more than enough money, so why should your father object to him so strongly?'

'Because he didn't go to a public school and he hasn't got a title. "Not our style at all, Janey luv. I want better than that for my little girl ...!" Wonderful, isn't it?' she added bitterly. 'Dad's a self-made man and has always professed to be proud of it.'

'It's often those sort of people who are the worst snobs,' Jane put in. 'If you're so much in love, why not just run away?'

'Ted won't agree to it without my father's consent.'

Although Jane considered this to be an unnecessarily idealistic outlook, she forbore to say so.

'Well then, what's wrong in waiting for a while?'

'Waiting?' It was a cry of outrage. 'You can't ever have

been in love to say such a thing! Anyway, even I was pre-pared to wait, Dad isn't. He's already got some witless sprig of the nobility lined up for me.' Tears trickled down her face and she brushed them away. 'I'm making a fool of myself. I'm sorry.'

'There's no need to cry. No one can make you marry someone if you don't want to.'

'You don't know my father.' The younger girl's voice was frightened. 'When anything stands in his way he can be ruthless. How many little men do you think have gone to the wall since he began to build up Belton's Bakeries? Suppose he decides to break Ted too?'

Jane did not reply, and unconsciously found herself look-ing round the hotel bedroom with its evidence of wealth. 'Could you be happy with a poor man?' she asked bluntly.

'If the man were Ted – yes. I'd rather marry him and have to scrub floors than marry some rich idiot.' The large eyes filled with tears. 'I hate to think what'd happen to me if I married a man I wasn't in love with. Can't you just see me in ten years? A gay divorcée with a series of boy-friends! Oh, Jane, I don't *want* to become that sort of person.'

'There's no reason why you should.'

'That's easy to say. I wouldn't want to *live* without Ted, and Dad won't even let us see each other. That's why I'm in London now – he's sending me on Dinky Howard's cruise. He says it'll help me to forget Ted.' She squeezed her hands together. 'The minute I'm away he'll try and persuade Ted to leave the country. He'll tell him it'll be for *my* good if he goes away.'

Jane frowned. 'I still don't see how I can help.'

'Don't you?' Janey looked at her with bright, alert eyes. 'Suppose you went on the cruise in *my* place? Nobody on the ship has met me, and if they do happen to have seen my picture, you're sufficiently like me to get away with it.'

'But I couldn't!'

'Why not? You wouldn't be doing anything criminal and you'd be getting a wonderful holiday into the bargain.'

12

Janey stood up and came closer. 'Why, Dinky's cruise is the most sought-after thing in the world.'

Jane's mind worked furiously. Mention of Dinky's name made her realize the significance of her position if she accepted this offer. Dinky Howard was doing everything in his power to keep the press out; what a scoop if she could go on board as a guest, if she could mingle with the socialites who were paying a fortune to have the reporters kept at bay!

Yet even though she saw the importance of the chance offered her, she was reluctant to accept it. To gain admittance to the ship for a few hours by a clever piece of acting was one thing; to pose for weeks on end as a different person, and use that pose in order to spy, was another.

'I don't feel I could do it,' she said slowly. 'And anyway, it wouldn't help to make your father change his mind.'

'At least I'd be here to make sure he doesn't send Ted away. I've a cousin in London and she knows Ted and likes him. I can stay with her until the cruise ends.' The younger girl clutched Jane's arm, her body trembling, tears pouring down her cheeks. 'You're my only hope. If you refuse me I won't have anything left to live for!'

'Don't say a thing like that!' Jane said sharply.

'But it's true. If Dad parts me from Ted I'll – I'll–'

The rest of Janey Belton's words were muffled by tears, and she flung herself on the bed, weeping. Jane watched in silence until she could bear it no longer.

'Please don't cry. If you really think it will help you then I'll – then I'll take your place.'

'Oh, you angel!' Janey was transfigured. 'I'll never be able to thank you enough.' She danced across to the dressing-table and began to repair her make-up. 'You'll have a wonderful time. The chance of going on a cruise like this doesn't come every day.'

'It certainly doesn't. I'd better be straight with you, Janey. If I go, it'll be as a reporter.'

The other laughed happily. 'I don't give a damn about that, so long as you go instead of me.'

Jane quelled her irritation. Despite her sympathy for the young heiress she could not help thinking her one of the most self-centred girls she had ever met.

'You might not give a damn, but what about the other guests? They might not object to giving a few interviews to the press, but they'd have a fit if they knew a reporter was watching them *all* the time.'

'Why are you telling me this?'

'Because it's only fair that you should know the score. From Mr. Howard's point of view I'm the worst possible choice.'

'Dinky Howard can look out for himself; he always has done.'

'Have you ever met him?'

'I told you. I've met no one at all who'll be on the cruise.' A giggle escaped her. 'Not even Lord Rupert Copinger.'

'Who's he?'

'The younger son of the Marquess of Dalcrosse.' Janey swept a mocking curtsey. 'The suitor Dad's got earmarked for me!'

'That's going to make it awkward, isn't it?'

'I don't see why. We've never met, and if he falls for you, you're welcome to him. His love mightn't last once he finds out who you are, so *you'd* better not fall for *him*!' Janey seized her shoulders and whirled her about the room. 'If you only knew how *happy* you've made me.'

'Take it easy,' Jane warned. 'Nothing's settled till I've spoken to my editor.'

'He's not likely to turn down the idea, is he?'

'Not unless his ulcers are bothering him! Now look, you'd better tell me how you propose to work this. Won't your father be coming to see you off?'

'No. He had to fly to Sweden for a conference. Bicks — that's the chauffeur — is calling for me tomorrow afternoon, so if you could be here at four, we'll drive to Southampton together. When we get there I'll get rid of him and you can go on board. Then I'll come back to London.'

'You've thought of everything, haven't you?'

'I only got the idea when I saw you this evening. I'm not usually so quick or efficient.'

'Perhaps you haven't had the chance to be!' Jane looked round for her bag. 'I'll have to fly. If my editor agrees I've got to do my packing and—'

'Don't bother packing,' Janey interrupted. 'You can take my clothes. I don't suppose you've anything suitable for a cruise.' Janey came close. 'You won't let me down, will you?'

'Don't worry,' Jane grinned. 'This is my big scoop!'

Her words were echoed by Frank Preston when she put the proposition to him. Delighted that she had wangled herself aboard the S.S. *Cambrian* he did not inquire too closely how she had managed it.

'It's a certainty none of the other papers will have anyone on board, so you'll have an exclusive. Cable us as often as you can and give us the lowdown on what's going on.'

'Won't it be dangerous to cable you?'

'I'm sure you'll be able to fix something with the wireless operator. That'll be a piece of cake compared with the trouble you must have had fixing yourself on board ship!' He leaned across the desk and patted her arm. 'Good luck, Jane. If Dinky finds out who you are, you'll be needing it!'

Jogging home in the bus, Jane wondered why Frank Preston's praise had given her a feeling of guilt. Why should she feel guilty because she had wangled a chance to go on the cruise? She had not lied or stolen to achieve it – indeed she was doing somebody a good turn.

She was still uneasy when she arrived home, and going into the kitchen she put the casserole, which the 'daily' had prepared, in the oven. Luckily her father had not yet returned and she went into the living-room and dialled the Saville Hotel. What she had to say to Janey Belton did not take long, and she was pale and shaken when she replaced the receiver, wishing she could forget the heiress's impassioned pleas to change her mind and not let her down.

Yet though she wished there were some way she could help the girl, Jane's main feeling was one of relief in the knowledge that she had done the right thing.

But what would Frank Preston say? Much though she had disliked ringing Janey, it was nothing to the fear she felt when her editor's voice came on the other end of the line. As quickly as she could she explained that she was not going on the cruise after all.

'How come it's fallen through?' he asked. 'When you left the office you seemed certain it was O.K. Do you need some more money as a bribe?'

'It's nothing like that,' Jane said quickly. 'It's just that I don't think it's ethical to go on the cruise and hide the fact that I'm a reporter. The passengers have paid a fortune for their privacy and—'

'Ethical!' The word exploded down the line. 'What's ethics got to do with it? Either you go on the cruise, or you look for another job!'

'But, Mr. Preston—'

'It's my last word, Jane. This was the biggest chance of your career, and if you're willing to turn it down then you'd do better to find yourself a job on *Kiddiewinks' Weekly*.'

The line went dead and she shakily replaced the receiver. Turning round, she saw her father in the doorway, and with an effort smiled at him.

'I didn't hear you come in, Dad. Caught any good crooks lately?'

'None worth mentioning.' Tom Berry removed his bowler and smoothed his forehead where the rim had left a red mark. 'I think I got more excitement on the beat than I do on this job.'

'You got less money too!'

'I know. But money isn't everything – if you'll forgive the cliché. The Metropolitan Insurance are a good firm, but it's not like working for the Yard.' He sniffed. 'Nice smell. I take it you haven't eaten yet?'

'No. I've only been in a few minutes. If you'd like to wash your hands and go into the dining-room I'll bring in the casserole.'

It was not until dinner was over and she and her father were sipping coffee that he asked her what had happened.

'I know something's up from the look on your face. Would I be wrong in assuming that a scoop's gone sour?'

'More than that,' she replied, and was glad their relationship was such that she could talk to him on equal terms. Trying to keep all emotion out of her voice, she told him what had happened.

'You'd have been a great help to Miss Belton if you *had* agreed to go,' he commented, as he stuffed tobacco into his pipe.

'Maybe so, but helping her would have meant letting down everybody else. I don't hold any brief for Dinky Howard, but the passengers go on his cruise in good faith.'

'If it's a question of good faith, then you're in the wrong job. I told you so when you went to work for that rag.'

'That "rag", as you call it, gives millions of people the news in a way they can understand,' Jane protested. 'Not everybody finds it easy to read *The Times*!'

'I won't argue with you about that. But I did warn you that ethics and the *Morning Star* don't go hand in hand.' Her father blew out a cloud of smoke. 'Beats me why Stephen Drake wanted to buy the *Morning Star*. It isn't as though he needs the money. His other interests bring in a fortune.'

'But they're all high class. Maybe he feels he's done a good thing in bringing the news to Mr. and Mrs. Average.'

'Mr. and Mrs. Moron, more likely,' her father grunted. 'There's no doubt—'

The ringing of the telephone cut him short and he picked it up. While he was talking Jane went into the kitchen to replenish their coffee cups, and by the time she returned her father was puffing at his pipe again.

'That cruise we were just discussing,' he said. 'Would you still be able to change your mind about it?'

'I should think so. Why?'

'Because I'd like you to ring Miss Belton and tell her you're willing to go.'

Jane stared at her father in astonishment. 'What's happened to all those ethics you were talking about a moment ago?'

'They still stand,' came the reply. 'Originally you were going on the cruise for the wrong reason; now I'm asking you to go for the *right* one.' Tom Berry stood up and began to pace the room. 'To have you on the *Cambrian* is the chance of a lifetime. It's the sort of thing that happens in T.V. serials, never in real life. When Marshall just told me ...'

Her father's voice trailed away, and Jane's curiosity mounted, for Dennis Marshall was a senior executive on the security side of the Metropolitan Insurance Company.

'You're making it sound very intriguing, Dad, but I've no intention of telling Janey or Mr. Preston that I've changed my mind unless you give a good reason for my doing so.'

'Would the Lorenz Diamond be a good enough reason?'

Jane's eyes widened. The stealing of the forty-carat diamond had hit the headlines of every paper less than a fortnight ago.

'You're not trying to tell me that it's on the ship?'

'That's exactly what I *am* trying to tell you. Unfortunately we don't know who's got it – only that it will be on board. According to our information it's being smuggled to Greece.'

'Pity your information couldn't tell you who was doing the smuggling.'

Her father sighed. 'Our informant is in the London Hospital at the moment – with his skull cracked. It's touch and go if he'll ever recover consciousness.'

Jane moistened her lips. 'I take it that it wasn't an accident?'

'No, it wasn't.'

'Even so, if you at least know the diamond will be on board, why don't you plant a detective there to keep watch on everyone?'

'Because Mr. Howard would refuse to allow us. The last thing in the word he wants is this sort of notoriety.'

'Why not send someone in the crew, or even as a passenger?'

'We've thought of that, but there isn't time. All the crew are hand-picked and there's no vacancy for another passenger. I suggested to Marshall that he tried to get one of the existing passengers to do a bit of snooping for us, but he won't hear of it. Insurance companies have to be very discreet.'

Jane grinned. 'I can imagine what the *Morning Star* editorial would say about it if they found out.'

'Exactly. That's why, when Marshall just rang and told me that the jewel was going to be on the *Cambrian*, I realized what a godsend this set-up of yours could be. You're the ideal person, Jane. You're intelligent, you know how to keep your eyes open, and besides that, no one will dream of suspecting Janey Belton of working for anyone except herself!'

The doorbell rang, and before Jane could answer it, her father was already in the hall. A moment passed and he came back holding a small parcel.

'When I told Marshall about your going on the cruise, he said you should have a look at this,' he told her.

'You took it for granted I'd change my mind, didn't you?'

'Naturally. I'm not interested in your story for the *Morning Star*, nor in helping the love life of a silly girl. But the Lorenz Diamond is worth a quarter of a million pounds and we've got to get it back.'

As he spoke he opened the parcel and took out a gold coin.

He put it on the palm of his hand and held it out for his daughter to see.

She stared down at it, intrigued by the strangely fashioned letter 'L' embossed on one side.

'What is it?' she asked.

'I suppose you could call it a talisman. The gang that carried out this job regarded it as their membership card. If you find the person on board who carries a coin like this, you'll be half-way to helping us find the diamond.'

'And what do I do if I *do* find them? Lock them in a cupboard and dial 999?'

Her father frowned. 'This isn't a joking matter, Jane. If you discover anything at all, tell the Captain at once. He'll know what to do. But on no account do anything on your own. If anything should happen to you . . .'

'Don't worry, Dad, I was only teasing. I'm sorry.' She took another careful look at the medallion. 'It's horrible to think that a lump of carbon can cause men to steal.'

'And murder,' her father reiterated. 'I doubt very much whether Hawton will recover.'

'If he *does* say anything else, will you let me know?'

'Of course. I'll cable you even if it's just the thinnest of clues. Every single bit of information you have to go on will be of help.' He lit his pipe again and settled back in his chair. 'Incidentally, no one must know what you're up to.'

'How can they? I'm going as an heiress.'

'I know that. But even if your real identity is found out – that you're a reporter, I mean – you mustn't tell a soul you're doing this job for us. It could be dangerous for you. Very dangerous.'

Although Jane thought her father was being over-serious she did not say so, and picking up the telephone dialled the number of the *Morning Star* and asked to be put through to the Features Editor.

'Mr. Preston,' she said in a voice shaking with suppressed excitement, 'it's Jane Berry here. I wanted to tell you I've

changed my mind. I'm willing to go on the cruise after all
. . . Yes, you were quite right. There's nothing more important than getting a good story.'

CHAPTER TWO

At four o'clock the following day Jane entered the suite occupied by the Belton heiress, and from the look of relief which flooded Janey's face it was obvious that until this moment she had experienced some doubt as to whether Jane would arrive at all.

'Thank goodness you've come,' she exclaimed. 'We must leave at once.' She thrust out a bunch of keys. 'You'd better take care of these from now on. There's no point arriving on board with a hundred dresses and no way of getting at them!'

Chattering excitedly, she led the way down in the lift and crossed the lobby to the entrance where a maroon and silver Rolls-Royce was waiting for them. As the car glided through the traffic Jane felt for the first time that her adventure was beginning, and she sat erect in the car and tilted her head imperiously as they passed a queue of people waiting for a bus. She was aware of envious and admiring glances and she suppressed a grin. So this was how the rich lived; there was a great deal to be said for it!

Janey fumbled in her bag and took out a bundle of letters. 'You'd better keep these too. They're the ones I've written to Dad. I've arranged them in date order, so all you need to do is to post them when you stop at a port. And you'd better take these as well.' She held out a passport and some travellers' cheques, but Jane shook her head.

'I've got my own passport and money, thanks.'

'Don't be silly. You can't use your own passport. You've got to take mine whether you like it or not.'

Secretly glad that no matter what she did to break the law it could easily be rectified by her father, Jane put the passport in her handbag.

'I won't take the cheques, though,' she said. 'If I start

forging your signature I really will begin to feel like a criminal.'

'All right.' The younger girl put the money away. 'If you want me for anything you can get in touch with me at my cousin's place – 1845 Park Street, Mayfair. But don't write unless you have to.' She stretched her arms above her head in a gesture of victory. 'I still can't believe it's happened. Can you imagine Ted's face when he finds out I'm still in England?'

Watching the young, wilful face in front of her, Jane wondered what sort of man Ted could be to bring such a look of happiness and vulnerability to it.

'What's he like?' she asked softly.

Janey smiled. 'You probably wouldn't give him a second look. He's not good-looking or sophisticated, but he's terribly kind.'

Jane was surprised that a girl of nineteen could rate kindness as the most important asset for a man. 'Not that it isn't,' she admitted to herself, but most of her contemporaries wanted something far more exciting than kindness!

'I suppose you've been in love dozens of times?' Janey asked. 'You must meet lots of men in your job.'

'Most of them are married. Not that that stops them from getting ideas! But thank goodness I've never fallen for one of them yet.'

'Don't you want to get married, or would you rather be a career girl?'

'There's no reason why the two can't go hand in hand,' Jane replied with some asperity. 'As it happens I've just not met anyone with whom I'd like to spend the rest of my life.'

She thought fleetingly of the many men she had dated in the past few years. Gay and amusing though most of them had been, none of them had engendered that extra *rapport* she considered so essential in a lasting relationship. Yet maybe she wasn't the sort of person ever to find a real relationship with anyone? The thought was so disquieting that

23

she pushed it to the back of her mind, angry with herself for allowing Janey's happiness to infect her in this way.

'Let's not talk about *me* any more,' she said. 'I'm supposed to be you, and I'd better know all the thing's you've got up to in the past few years.'

'It's all in the press cuttings. You should have read them.'

'I did! But there are still more facts I'd like to know. What are your favourite foods, for example, and what's your taste in music and art and literature?'

'I've got no taste in anything,' came the answer. 'I'm a nothing personality! Dad never gave me the chance to develop, and expensive boarding schools don't encourage you to be anything other than a conformist. So your task isn't difficult, Jane. Just be ordinary!'

It was six o'clock when they arrived at Southampton Docks and drew up at the quay where the s.s. *Cambrian* was moored. A flock of white-coated stewards waited to greet the passengers, and within a moment of Janey's cases being unloaded, they were cleared through the Customs and taken on board.

'Don't bother to wait,' the heiress instructed her chauffeur.

'I'd like to see you on board, miss,' he replied. 'Your father instructed me to do so.'

'Don't be stuffy, Bicks! Miss Berry's here and she'll make sure I don't run away.'

The man touched his cap, and returned to the car.

'I hope your father won't blame him for all this,' Jane murmured.

'Dad would never sack Bicks. He's the only chauffeur who can stick him!' She grinned at Jane. 'I've five minutes to catch the London train and I'll just do it. I'll see you when you come back. I know you'll have a wonderful time and I'm sure you won't regret it.'

'I hope not,' Jane answered, and watched as the girl threaded her way through the crowds and disappeared towards the station. Then with a deep breath she walked up the gangplank and, handing over her passport and tickets, stepped on board.

The moment she did so she seemed to be in another world; a floating planet where luxury was taken for granted. Two stewards stepped forward; one took her bag and hold-all, the other her coat, then they escorted her up a flight of stairs to the main deck and down a panelled corridor carpeted in red. Half-way along they stopped and, unlocking a door, ushered her into a stateroom whose magnificence took her breath away. Just in time she bit back an exclamation of delight; it would never do for the Belton heiress to be over-awed by her surroundings.

'The far door leads into the bathroom,' one of the stewards said, 'and those two bells by your bed should give you all the service you require. One is for your personal maid and the other for the steward. The phone will connect you to any other part of the world.'

The door closed behind them and, left alone, Jane allowed her curiosity full vent. How stupid to have expected an ordinary ship's cabin! This room was even larger than her bedroom at home, and its fittings more worthy of a palace than a ship.

Taking off her coat, she flung it on the marble-topped table and sank down on the small love seat placed near the porthole. The scent from a basket of flowers on the dressing-table tickled her nostrils, and from sheer excitement she jumped up again and pirouetted round the room. 'It's the opportunity of a lifetime, Jane Berry,' she told herself, and then caught her breath. She was Jane Berry no longer. She was Janey Belton, and she had better become used to thinking of herself in this way.

'I'm Janey Belton,' she whispered aloud. 'My father's head of Belton's Bakeries and I'm worth a million. I'm used to mink and diamonds, and I'm bored to death with smoked salmon and caviare!'

Feeling she was finally putting aside her identity, she

took off her things and hung them in the back of the wardrobe. Although the steward had said a maid would attend to her needs, she decided to unpack for herself; at least it would give her the opportunity to see everything she had at her disposal. She unlocked the four white pigskin cases and flung back the lids, catching her breath in delight as she took out one beautiful dress after another.

It was not until she opened what she took to be a vanity case that she realized there were jewels to go with each outfit too. And what jewels! Never in her life had she seen such diamonds or pearls, and she had certainly never held anything in her grasp as exquisite as the flower spray of rubies, sapphires and emeralds. Hastily she put all the jewellery away and locked the vanity case. She might have to wear Janey's clothes, but nothing would induce her to wear any of these valuable trinkets. Horror at what would happen were she to lose one of them made her slip on her dress and hurry down to the Purser's office. She handed over the case to him and watched with relief as he placed it in a locker and handed her the key.

Returning to her stateroom, Jane put the clothes away and then relaxed in a warm bath. Even the bathroom was bigger than her own bedroom, and peach-tinted mirrors lined the walls and gave back myriad reflections of her figure. In such surroundings it was difficult not to be aware of herself, and as she reached for a towel she could not help appreciating the graceful line of her shoulders and thighs.

Fashion writers might say that youth and beauty needed no adornment, but when, fully dressed some half-hour later, she stared at her reflection in the full-length mirror in her stateroom, she realized how untrue this was. Always considered to be a pretty girl, Jane now looked radiant in a long dress of hyacinth chiffon lightly spattered with pink roses.

With careful hands she applied her usual amount of make-up, but somehow the discreet application of lipstick and mascara seemed insufficient and she had the fanciful notion that the dress would come in for more comment than she would herself. It was as if the thing had a life of its own!

'Probably because I know it must have cost about a hundred and fifty pounds,' she murmured. 'If I'm not careful thse damned clothes will give me an inferiority complex!'

Luckily there was a complete make-up kit in Janey's luggage, and though Jane had put it to one side, not expecting to use it, she retrieved it from the bottom of the wardrobe and set it out on the dressing table. Thoughtfully she stared at the little pots and tubes, and then, deciding that in for a penny in for a pound, she proceeded to make up her face the way she had seen Maggie do it so many times in the office.

The result made Jane feel even more of a stranger to herself, but she was none the less delighted at the added confidence it gave her. 'Maybe I'd have got a few more scoops if I'd tried this before,' she thought cynically, and peering at her face closely in the glass fluttered her long eyelashes up and down.

Only her hair had been left in its normal fashion, falling soft and blonde to her shoulders, the ends curling gently outwards. In normal circumstances it made her appear young and unsophisticated, yet now, allied to heavier make-up, it gave her a provocative look of innocence belied by the blue-lidded, almond-shaped eyes and the pouting red mouth.

's.s *Cambrian*, here I come!' she said out loud, and picking up a blue evening bag, closed the stateroom door behind her.

Only as she reached the lower deck and the dining-room did her nervousness return and she stood hesitantly at the entrance, wondering which was her table.

The *maître* hurried forward to greet her. 'I am delighted to welcome you on board, Miss—'

'Janey Belton.'

The man glanced at the list in his hand. 'Ah, so. You are sitting with some delightful people. Of course, if you care to change later, just tell me and I will see to it at once.'

27

Jane lowered her eyelids in a supercilious way and followed him to a table at one side of the dining-room. Many admiring glances followed her, but none more admiring than that of the slim, fair-haired man sitting next to a middle-aged couple, whose admiration changed to positive disbelief as the *maître* stopped in front of him and held out the vacant chair.

Introductions were made, and Jane sat down, making a pretence of studying her menu. As the *maître* murmured the names of her dining companions she was glad of her newspaper background, for she had been immediately able to place them. The middle-aged couple were Sir Brian and Lady Pendlebury. He was the first baronet and had acquired his title through the charitable use of money which he had acquired in less pleasant ways. His first wife had been discarded by the wayside and the present Lady Pendlebury came of impecunious but landed gentry.

The fair-haired man was Colin Waterman, a playboy whose name figured prominently in the Society columns. She remembered that his father had been killed when he was a child and that he had been brought up by his mother, an extravagant woman who had frittered away a great deal of money. Not all the money, though, Jane thought, for Colin Waterman was still considered an eligible catch and was to be seen at all the big functions.

His glance of admiration was more expressive than words, and Jane coloured. She was glad when Lady Pendlebury joined in the conversation and discussion was general for the rest of the meal. She was amused at the way Sir Brian tucked into his food; he obviously believed that what he paid for must be eaten, and he tackled everything with the gusto of a starving man. Something of what she felt must have been apparent in her face, for as she caught Colin Waterman's eye he grinned.

'Been to the Zoo lately, Miss Belton?' he asked conversationally.

Jane choked on the wine she was sipping, but Sir Brian

and his wife did not raise their eyes from their plates, and she breathed a sigh of relief and gave the young man a reproachful look.

He continued to grin back at her unabashed, and she could not help warming to him.

It was not until she was eating a mouth-watering soufflé that she glanced round the room, wondering which one of the men could be Janey's suitor. For the most part the people were middle-aged, although in the far corner there was a younger group, their loud laughter and chatter causing her to remember Maggie's remark about 'high-pitched voices and chi-chi'.

The conversation seemed to be dominated by a slim, elegant girl with dark hair who, glancing across the room, noticed Jane's stare and responded to it with a haughty look. Hastily Jane averted her eyes.

'I suppose you know lots of people on board,' Colin Waterman said.

'I don't recognize anyone,' Jane said carefully. 'I spend most of my time in a small town, and my father doesn't like me racketing around.'

'Not even in your pretty red sports car?' As he saw her look of astonishment, the young man's pale eyes crinkled. 'You figure in the gossip columns almost as much as I used to do, Miss Belton. Which reminds me, we can't go on calling each other Mr. and Miss all the time, so let's make it Janey and Colin.'

She nodded and relaxed a little. 'I suppose *you* know everyone here.'

'Quite a lot of them – which is one of the reasons I came on the cruise. It's easier to relax among people you know. If you go to the usual holiday places they're jam-packed with tourists and working girls on the prowl for rich husbands.'

Jane bit back an angry retort. 'How right you are,' she drawled. 'I've had exactly the same experience – in reverse, of course. So many men are just fortune-hunters.'

Colin grinned. 'Well, you can relax for the next couple of

weeks at least, and give nightly thanks to Dinky Howard.'

'Where is he, by the way? I've never met him.'

'He doesn't come into the dining-room often, and when he does you'll find him at the Captain's table with the richer of the millionaires.'

Jane laughed. 'I never thought millionaires needed qualifying.'

'They certainly do.' There was a dry humour in Colin's light voice. 'Millionaire, multi-millionaire, Greek shipping tycoon, oil sheikh and rich Texan.'

'The last one being a masterly understatement, I take it?'

He nodded. 'Right in one. It's a pleasure having a quick dinner companion.' He pushed back his chair. 'Would you like to have coffee with me in the ballroom? There's no dancing yet, but it's pleasant to sit there.'

'I'd love to.'

She followed him out of the dining-room and noticed that he acknowledged greetings from a great many people, and in particular the occupants of the table she had noticed a few moments earlier.

'What a pretty dark-haired girl,' she remarked. 'Her face is awfully familiar. Who is she?'

'Claire Saunders. She was the most famous deb of her year about ten years ago.'

The name brought to mind all the stories Jane had heard about her; a poor little rich girl whose escapades had landed her on the front page of most of the tabloids a few years ago. There had been rumours that she had run through most of her money, but she still seemed to dress as well as ever and her name was linked frequently with middle-aged industrialists.

As they sipped their coffee in the ballroom and listened to a pianist soulfully playing Gershwin melodies, Jane studied her escort carefully, revising her earlier opinion that he was just a pleasant young man. His drawling way of speaking was merely a sign of public school education, but beneath it he had an agile mind and a slightly waspish sense of humour. He was not the sort of young man she could relax with, for he would be quick to spot any discrepancies in her story.

'Dinky Howard told me you were coming on this cruise,' Colin interrupted her thoughts. 'Generally he's pretty tight-mouthed about the people who are going to be on board.'

'Then why does he send the passenger list to all the newspapers?'

Colin looked surprised. 'Does he do that? I didn't know.'

Jane bit her lip. 'I only found out because I – because a reporter came to see me the other day and mentioned it.'

'You should know better than to give interviews to reporters. They're the biggest liars in the world!'

'That wasn't my impression of them. They're just people doing a job of work.'

'You *are* innocent, aren't you?'

Sensing the conversation could lead her into difficulties, Jane did what she thought Janey Belton would have done in the same circumstances, and gave a little giggle before changing the subject.

'What do you do when you're not on holiday, Colin?'

'Nothing. I made up my mind years ago that I didn't want to work. Life is so short it seems a pity to spend one's time amassing money that one doesn't need.'

'So you spend it instead.'

'Exactly!'

'But aren't you bored doing nothing?'

'I haven't time to be bored. I play polo, I water-ski, I paint—'

'But they're all hobbies.'

The pale eyes looked at her blankly. 'What do *you* do, Janey? Don't tell me you've got the urge to find a job?'

Jane wondered what he would say if she told him the truth, and looked forward to the end of the cruise when she would be able to do so.

'It's different for a girl,' she said lamely. 'And anyway, I – I keep house for my father.'

'Which one of his houses?'

She giggled and thanked her lucky stars that she had carefully read the press cuttings Frank Preston had given her.

'All three of them.'

'Colin, you beast, why didn't you come and say hello to me?'

Jane looked up to see Claire Saunders beside their table. At close range she was even more beautiful than Jane had expected, and it was not only a beauty that came from exquisite clothes and grooming, but from her startling colouring and haughty carriage. She was certainly not completely English, for her milk-white skin, blue-black hair and the imperious way she had of turning her head and flashing her brown eyes spoke more for the Spanish aristocrat than the English rose.

Colin stood up and introduced the two girls.

'Sorry I didn't come over, Claire, but you seemed pretty occupied.'

'I'm never too occupied to talk to you, darling,' the girl replied. Her accent and manner were almost identical with Colin's and Jane felt as though she was looking at a different species of beings.

'Is this the first time you've been on one of Dinky's cruises?' Claire spoke directly to her.

'Yes. Have you been on them before?'

'Lots of times. They're quite fun generally, but this one seems as if it's going to be deadly dull.'

'I hope present company's excepted,' Colin said gently.

'Oh, darling, don't be touchy! I just meant that everyone else looks so stodgy. There's not one dynamic—' Her voice trailed away as her eyes came to rest on the glass doors that led out to the promenade deck. They were swinging quickly as though they had been violently pushed by the tall, heavy-shouldered man standing in front of them.

Even at a distance it was impossible not to be aware of his

magnetism, and though his features could not be clearly seen, Jane had an impression of tanned skin and hair as black as Claire's own.

'Well, well,' Claire drawled. 'Now that really is something. Do you know who he is, Colin?'

'No.' Colin frowned and there was a strange hesitancy in his voice. 'He wasn't on the list a few days ago.'

Jane looked at him in surprise, wondering why he had expressed surprise when she herself had mentioned the passenger list a short while ago. But both Colin and Claire were watching the tall dark man make his way to a table and, sitting down, bury his head in a book.

'He obviously hasn't come on this cruise with any sociable intent,' Jane said.

'The poor man's probably afraid of being overwhelmed.' Claire took a gold cigarette case out of her handbag and lit a cigarette. She did not offer them round and, watching her, Jane was sure her mind was miles away. Seen in repose, her face did not look as young as Jane had first assumed. The girl must be in her late twenties, almost an old maid according to débutante standards! Yet this fact could surely only be one of choice, for it was difficult to believe she had not received many proposals of marriage. Perhaps she had never fallen in love? Jane watched as the dark eyes studied the man sitting at the other end to the room, and she knew that if Claire was still unattached at the end of the cruise it would not be of her own choice.

She stifled a yawn and pushed back her chair. 'I think I'll go to bed, if you'll excuse me. It's been a long day and I'm tired.'

'I'll see you down to your cabin,' Colin said.

'Don't bother, thanks. It's silly to stand on ceremony on a ship.'

She made her way out of the ballroom and, once on the deck, breathed deeply of the cool air. She walked over to the ship's side and leaned on the rail, staring down at the onyx-like water which, below the cloud-covered sky, gave off no reflection except its own. She stood there for a long time, only becoming aware of her surroundings again when she breathed in the smell of a Havana cigar. Turning, she saw a man half hidden in the shadows. He too was leaning on the rail and as she watched he tossed the end of his cigar over the side.

'What a pity you've come to the end of it,' she said. 'I love the smell.'

He turned sharply in her direction, and as he did so a dim light coming from one of the curtained staterooms fell upon his face. At once she recognized him as the man Claire Saunders had pointed out. He was even more good-looking than she had expected, though perhaps good-looking was the wrong word, for his features were too decisive, the nose too prominent, the mouth too large. Yet it was the sort of commanding and powerful face that a woman would be attracted by.

'If I'd known you were there,' he said, his voice courteous but aloof, 'I'd have inhaled more slowly. But I thought everyone was happily drinking and talking.'

'I was on my way to bed,' she explained, 'but the evening was so beautiful I couldn't bear to go inside. I love the nighttime,' she confided. 'It's so different and – and somehow full of space.'

'If it's space you're interested in you shouldn't have come on this trip. As far as I can see it's going to be absolute hell. You can't walk a yard without falling over someone!'

She looked at him in astonishment, wondering whether he meant his remark to be so rude. As she saw his rigid face she knew he was fully aware of what he had said and that he did not care what implications she drew from it.

'It seems you're the one who's made the mistake,' she said coldly. 'People who come on a holiday like this do so because they're gregarious.'

'Nonsense. They merely like the opportunity of parading their clothes and jewels and letting their back hair down without fear of hitting the headlines.'

'If it isn't a rude question,' she retorted, 'perhaps you'd care to tell me why *you're* here?'

'I've been asking myself the same question all evening.' He rubbed the side of his face and smiled ruefully. It made him look disarmingly young, and some of her anger abated. 'Anyway, I can see I've offended you. I'm sorry that you've taken my remarks personally.'

'They seemed rather personal.'

'I didn't mean them to be. I apologize again, Miss—'

'Belton. Janey Belton.'

He gave a slight bow. 'I'm Stephen Drake.'

'Stephen Drake!' she echoed his name, too taken aback to say more. What a horrible mischance that he of all people should be on this cruise. The millionaires and oil tycoons Colin had blithely mentioned she could easily have taken in her stride, but not Stephen Drake, who controlled one of the largest newspaper chains in the country and who was, though he did not know it, her boss!

She made a move to run past him, but as she did so the engines throbbed more loudly beneath her feet and the sound suddenly made her remember whom she was supposed to be. As far as Stephen Drake was concerned she was not a lowly reporter who worked for him but Janey Belton, an heiress who did not fear any man, no matter what his position or power.

With a sigh she relaxed and studied him curiously, conscious of the pull of his personality. He was younger than the half-scowling pictures she had seen of him, and there was humour in the dark, narrow eyes beneath their thick black brows. There was certainly something to be said for travelling incognito, she thought, and a gleam came into her eyes as she determined to exploit her position to the full and get to know this man who was watching her with such a sardonic expression.

'Well,' he said, his thin mouth lifting, 'do I meet with your approval?'

'I'm sorry. I didn't know I was staring.'

35

'It's a habit of the young,' he said. 'And now if you'll excuse me I'm going to find a little bit of that space you were talking about a moment ago. Good night, Miss Beaton.'

Bowing slowly, he turned on his heel, and Jane watched him go, her face mirroring her chagrin.

'Beaton!' she exclaimed. 'He knows perfectly well it's Belton. What an arrogant man.' She tilted her head defiantly. 'I'd love the chance of bringing him to heel!'

CHAPTER THREE

In her first waking moments Jane could not remember where she was and stared, puzzled, at the swaying curtains that covered the round windows of her bedroom.

Round windows? All at once she remembered where she was and sat up in bed, aware of the swelling movement of the ship. Gingerly she pushed aside the bedclothes and stepped on to the floor.

Standing up, the movement was more noticeable, and she padded over to the porthole and looked in dismay at the turbulent grey sea. So much for the sunshine cruise!

It needed care to wash and dress, for the water in the bath had a habit of slopping on the floor when the ship tilted, and looking at her swaying reflection in the mirror she knew herself lucky to be feeling no ill effects.

'I wonder how many other passengers have got their sea-legs,' she thought, and found the answer as she entered the deserted dining-room for breakfast.

A young waiter, busy polishing cutlery, came over to her.

'Would you be wanting breakfast, miss?'

'Yes, please. Or am I too late?'

'You're about an hour too early, I'd say. Most of the passengers don't breakfast until nine, and then they take it in their cabins.'

A quick glance at her watch showed Jane it was barely eight o'clock, and she was annoyed with herself for not realizing that the sort of girl she was supposed to be would never have risen at such an early hour and, once risen, would certainly not traipse down to the dining-room. But it was too late to do anything about it now, and she looked round for a table that was already laid.

'If you wouldn't mind sitting at the other side of the room,' the waiter said deferentially. 'We only prepare a few tables for breakfast. Though from the look of the weather I shouldn't think we'll have to provide many more for lunch either!'

He led the way across the floor to a small alcove at the end where a round table was set with yellow breakfast crockery. She saw she was not the only one who had come down to breakfast, for it was already occupied by a black-haired, saturnine man who was sipping his coffee and reading a newspaper. Stephen Drake!

Hesitantly she stood by the chair and he looked up and saw her. An expression of chagrin matching her own crossed his face as he stood up, and she debated whether to ask the waiter to lay a place for her at another table.

Before she could do so Stephen Drake spoke.

'Would you mind very much sitting down? My breakfast is getting cold.'

Reddening, she did so, and he resumed his seat and continued eating. Jane ordered coffee and toast, and while she waited for it wished she had had the foresight to bring a book with her; even a menu would have been a help, for she could have studied it instead of having to stare vacantly into space.

To her relief the waiter arrived with her order and she busied herself pouring coffee. Her companion had still not lifted his head from his paper and her anger rose at his bad manners.

'Darn the man,' she thought furiously, 'why should I allow him to get under my skin?' Determined to show him she did not care if he sat as silent as a Buddha, she signalled the waiter and asked him to bring her a morning paper.

'I'm afraid we won't be getting any until we call at the next port. There's a ship's paper, of course, but I'm not sure what time it'll be available. I'll go and inquire for you.'

As the waiter walked away, Stephen Drake put down his copy of *The Times* and looked at her.

'This is yesterday's, I'm afraid. I'd have offered to share it with you, but I didn't think you'd find it interesting reading. There aren't many pictures in it.'

'I don't mind a few words too,' she said sweetly, 'provided they aren't too difficult.'

For an instant he looked taken aback, then a glint of humour became visible in the dark eyes.

'Lord,' he said, 'I must have sounded insufferably patronizing. It's just that I'm so used to women preferring the tabloids. And if you'll forgive my saying so, you're much too pretty to bother your head with this sort of stuff.' He tapped the paper in front of him. 'But you're very welcome to take it – as long as you don't mind yesterday's news.'

'I don't mind at all,' she said. '*The Times* of yesterday is better than the *Morning Star* of today.'

It was as though a shutter came down over his face, and Jane regretted her impulsiveness.

'I'm sorry,' she said. 'Now *I'm* the one who's rude. It's just that I – I know who you are and I was trying to be funny.'

His thick eyebrows lifted. 'The only thing funny about your remark is that you should know who I am. Most people don't.'

'I read about you in the *Morning Star* a few years ago. It was when you bought the paper.'

She did not add that at that time she had also made up her mind to work on it, and wondered what he would say were he to discover she was an employee of his. She bit her lip to hide a smile. If only Maggie could see her now, sharing a breakfast table and the marmalade pot with Fleet Street's biggest tycoon!

'It must be wonderful being in such a position of power,' she said artlessly. 'I suppose you've got plans to become bigger and bigger?'

'I haven't any plans at all at the moment. I'm too tired.'

'Tired! You strike me as much too dynamic ever to be tired.'

'Even a dynamo can run down,' he sighed. 'At least, that's what the doctor chaps have been telling me for the past few months.'

He rubbed the side of his face, a gesture she had seen him do once before, only this time she realized it was not a mannerism but a sign of exhaustion. It could explain the lines on his face and the shadows round his eyes.

'People don't understand that having to exercise power can drain you of all your vitality,' he went on. 'They assume that once you've reached the top the rest is easy.'

'I'd say that staying at the top is even tougher than getting there,' she answered. 'When you've nothing to lose, it isn't as much strain as when you've everything to lose just by making one false move.'

'And yet it's the knowledge that you can lose everything by one mistake that makes power so exciting.' He leaned forward, his body tense. 'Being the biggest man in your field without any competition to worry you is like a living death. The only thing that makes life worth anything at all is the danger in it, the knowledge that it's *you* against everyone else. Ordinary routine business is like a—' he hesitated – 'like a casserole cooked without seasoning!'

'And you regard danger as the *bouquet garni*?'

He laughed. 'For a sheltered heiress you display great understanding.'

It was too late to revert to ingenuousness, and she had to see the conversation through.

'Just because my father's Cedric Belton it doesn't make me an idiot!'

'My dear child, I wasn't for the moment suggesting you were. I was merely remarking that it's unusual for a girl in your position to be so intelligent.'

'I suppose you think only career women are intelligent?'

'Unfortunately yes. It's rare to find an intelligent woman who's content to stay in the background.' There was a bleakness in his voice she could not help noticing. 'Female emancipation has been a terrible thing for men. If a woman today has any capabilities she regards keeping house and bearing children and taking care of her husband as a bore and a nuisance. She has to go into the man's world and compete against him. She has to prove she can be as good as he is, and yet uses every feminine wile to do so!'

Intuition told Jane he was speaking from experience, and she wished she knew more about his past life. Was he divorced? Had he been in love with a woman who had given him up in place of a career? She longed to ask him, yet knew that even in the guise of the artless Janey Belton she could not do so.

The waiter came into the alcove carrying a couple of sheets of newsprint in his hand. 'Hot off the press,' he grinned, and handed them each a copy of the *Cambrian News.*

Jane glanced at it. It was mostly social chit-chat about the passengers, and she recognized Dinky Howard's verbose style in the prose. There was little mention of the news in England, but as she turned the sheet over her eye was caught by a black headline half-way down the page. 'ONE-TIME JOCKEY DIES IN LONDON HOSPITAL.' Her body stiffening, Jane read on. 'Edward Hawton, who in his youth was a well-known steeplechase jockey, died in the early hours of the morning of injuries received in a road accident two days ago. The driver of the car did not stop, and Mr. Hawton, who only recovered consciousness for a couple of moments, was unable to give the police any clue.'

Jane put down the paper. This must be the man her father had told her about, the one he had hoped would be able to give them more evidence as to the whereabouts of the Lorenz Diamond. She wondered whether, in the few moments of consciousness, Hawton had been able to say anything further.

'Bad news?' With a start she looked up to see Stephen Drake watching her intently.

'I was just – I was just reading about someone who was killed in a hit-and-run accident.'

'Hawton, you mean? Yes, I was looking at that a moment

ago. Poor devil. He was a wonderful rider in his time. I used to watch him.'

'Did you know him?'

'Vaguely. You couldn't be a racegoer and not know him.' He crumpled his napkin and stood up. 'I expect I'll be seeing you again, Miss Belton. If you haven't succumbed to *malaise* by now, you've obviously got your seagoing legs.'

She watched him disappear through the alcove and then poured herself another cup of coffee, thoughtfully staring into space as she remembered their conversation.

When Jane returned to her cabin she found a note from Colin pushed through the door. He wrote that he was in bed with no hope of getting up until the weather was calmer, but looked forward to seeing her as soon as the sun shone again.

It was a friendly note and it warmed her to feel there was at least one other person on the ship who was human. She thought again of her breakfast companion. He was a man of intensity and dynamism, of that there was no doubt, but whether or not he was human was another question.

Luckily Janey had equipped her wardrobe for all weathers, and Jane put on a thick ribbed lemon wool coat, tied a pale green headscarf round her hair and went up to the top deck. The moment she stepped out of the shelter of the companionway the wind tore at her with fierce fingers and she was buffeted along the deck, arriving breathless at the prow. She was able to obtain shelter by standing beside a mound of chairs covered with waterproof and lashed safely together with stout rope, and from this vantage point gazed out at the foaming sea and grey sky. Loath to return to the stuffy interior of the ship, for even air-conditioning was stuffy compared with the salty tang of sea air, she decided to remain on deck, and pulled at the ropes in order to release one of the chairs. They were damp with moisture and her fingers slipped, her knuckles grazing against the wood. She gave an exclamation of pain and pressed them against her mouth.

'Let me do it for you.'

She looked up, surprised to see Stephen Drake. Heavens! The man would think she was chasing him if they kept meeting so often.

'I – I didn't know you were here.'

'I've been standing on the other side of the deck-chairs.' He smiled briefly. 'If you want to watch the sea this is the only sheltered part to do it from.'

'I didn't realize that. I don't want to be in your way, but I – I would like to sit down.'

'My dear girl, there's no reason why you shouldn't. The yacht isn't mine, you know.'

'Last night you said you wanted to be alone.'

'Last night I also apologized for being rude.'

He turned his attention to the chairs and deftly undid the ropes. He placed two against the shelter of the wall and then disappeared through a door on the left which she had not noticed, re-emerging with two brightly coloured blankets.

Ignoring her protests, he pushed her into the chair and wrapped the blanket firmly around her legs, pushing it up until it nestled beneath her chin. He did the same for himself and they were soon sitting cocooned in wool, side by side.

He made no conversation and seemed content to gaze out to sea, occasionally closing his eyes and drifting off into sleep. During these moments Jane watched him with unabashed curiosity, aware of how different his face looked in repose. There was no doubt that the excitement he had talked about earlier that morning had taken its toll of him, for though she had a vague remembrance that he was about thirty-five, he looked considerably older. Yet he still remained the most attractive-looking man she had ever met.

The morning passed quickly and at noon the deck steward approached them with hot consommé. Though she had assumed the man by her side to be asleep, he sat up straight the moment the steward approached.

'I didn't mean to wake you, sir.'

'You didn't, but I'm a light sleeper.' Stephen Drake took

43

the consommé and sipped it appreciatively. 'I hope I haven't been snoring, Miss Belton?'

'Even if you had I wouldn't tell you.'

'A very well brought up little girl.'

'I'm not a little girl. I'm—' Jane was almost going to say twenty-three, but remembered in time that she was only supposed to be nineteen.

'Well?' he teased. 'How old *are* you?'

'Nineteen.'

'You look about fifteen with that scarf on and that fluffy wool thing you're wearing.'

'This fluffy wool thing is a Givenchy!'

'That just shows how lucky you are.'

Remembering Janey's domination by her father, Jane could not help replying:

'It isn't always lucky to inherit money. You said power brings problems. Well, so does wealth.'

'You surprise me. I should have thought the only problem you have is deciding which suitor to accept.'

'And also deciding which suitor loves me and not Belton's Bakeries.'

'Ah, yes, I was forgetting.' His face was sympathetic. 'That must be quite a problem to you. Still, I'm sure there are plenty of wealthy young men you can choose from.'

'What about you?' Jane said with daring. 'I'm sure there are lots of wealthy young girls *you* can choose too. Or are you already married?'

'No, I'm not. And I've no intention of ever getting married either. I was – I was engaged some time ago, and when it ended I decided to stick to business.'

Jane looked at him with innocent eyes. 'Was she a pretty, dumb blonde like me, or was she an intelligent career woman?'

'You've got a very inquiring mind, haven't you?'

'I'm sorry,' she said quickly. 'I'm curious about people and – and it's an awful habit of mine to ask point-blank questions.'

44

'You'd make a good reporter,' he said dryly. 'If ever you decide to take a job, come and see me.'

She giggled. 'Would you give me one?'

'As a matter of fact, no. You're not tough enough for Fleet Street.'

Jane's temper rose but she managed not to answer him back.

'I don't think you'd have called Georgina pretty,' he said unexpectedly.

Jane realized he was answering her question and she waited for him to continue, hoping that what he said would give her some clue as to his emotional life.

'Striking was a better word for her. She was taller than you, with jet black hair and brown eyes.'

A picture of Claire Saunders flashed into Jane's mind. 'Was she English?'

'No, American. She was working for a magazine in London and I met her when I took over the group.'

'So she was working for you.'

'Yes.'

'What went wrong?'

He was so long replying that she was afraid this time she had gone too far, and in order to show him that she was not expecting an answer she closed her eyes, surprised when she heard his voice again.

'Georgina only saw me in terms of my possessions and the power I wielded. As my wife she felt she would share them too. I didn't happen to agree with her and so – and so she went back to the States. She married a few months ago. Someone with a chain of small-town newspapers. I'm sure Georgina will turn it into a national concern before long.'

Jane opened her eyes. 'I'm sorry. No wonder you're so bitter against career women.'

'Did I tell you that?' He looked surprised. 'Lord, I seem to have talked a hell of a lot to you today. That's what comes of being on board ship. It makes everything else seem unreal.'

'That's why doctors recommend it. It's the quickest way of escaping from your problems.'

'I hope you're right. I can do with escaping from mine. Sometimes I think I never want to go back at all, that I'd like to live the life of a lotus eater on a Fijian island.'

He glanced at his watch and stood up. 'I'm going to have a work-out in the gymnasium before lunch. Maybe we'll meet again at dinner.'

Jane nodded and watched him stride away. In a few words he had given her a key to his character. Strange how simple were the reasons for one's complexities and yet how great were the repercussions they had on one's life. She was convinced that a broken love had given Stephen Drake the impetus to get to the top in the same way that it would also prevent him from allowing himself to fall in love again. Yet love did not know the meaning of the word allow; it was an emotion which, like the sea, could seep into the most tightly closed confines.

Determined not to give Stephen Drake a chance to think she was eager for his companionship, she deliberately did not go up to the top deck during the afternoon, but remained in the ship's lounge listening to a recorded musical concert. The weather had not improved and the ship creaked and groaned as it was tossed like a cork on the sea.

How awful if the weather remained like this the whole time! If the other passengers were closeted in their cabins it would put paid to her sending any stories to the *Morning Star*. Remembering the *Morning Star* made her realize she had not yet made any plans for sending her copy, and her earlier intention of trying to bribe the wireless operator did not seem such a good one now that she was actually on board. From what she had seen of the crew they were a hand-picked selection, and Dinky Howard was no doubt paying them sufficient to commandeer their loyalty. Anyway, her father had sworn her to secrecy about her identity, and if she were to cable news to the *Morning Star* it would mean breaking her promise. But this was something she dared not do, for memory of Hawton's death made her realize the significance of her father's warning. Which one of the passengers could be the man she wanted? Or perhaps it might even be a woman? From the little she had seen of everyone, no one seemed a likely candidate. 'If only I had another clue to go on,' she said to herself. 'Short of inspecting every bag and looking through every pocket for a gold coin, I don't see what I can do.'

Taking out a notebook from her handbag she scribbled down a description of the sumptuous furnishings of the *Cambrian*. If she could not find any gossip, she would at least be able to cable something descriptive to Frank Preston when the ship docked at Cannes.

Slowly the rest of the day dragged on and she was glad when she could return to her cabin and change for dinner. The weather was a little better, and when she entered the dining-room at eight-thirty it was about a quarter full. With a tingle of excitement she wondered whether Stephen Drake would suggest she sat with him, but as she walked towards her table she saw from the corner of her eye that he was already half-way through his meal.

As soon as she had finished her sweet she went up to the saloon and ordered coffee. What would Janey do in similar circumstances? she thought as she sipped it. One thing was certain: she would not sit here moping by herself but would go in search of excitement. 'But I'm not Janey Belton,' Jane admitted soberly, 'and I've neither the nerve nor the inclination to do anything except go to bed.'

She stood up, clutching hold of the back of her chair as the ship suddenly sloped to an alarming angle. The swell had increased considerably and she walked carefully down the corridor, gripping the rail that ran along one side of the wall. Even so it was difficult to keep her balance, for not only was the ship rocking from side to side, but it had started to pitch. The unusual motion made her feel light-headed and she stood still and closed her eyes, waiting for the nausea to pass. It seemed to steady momentarily and she

47

made a dash for the stairs, colliding with a man coming up them. Mortified, she recognized Stephen Drake!

'Not again!' she gulped. 'I'm always bumping into you.'

He looked at her in surprise, then seeing the paleness of her face he caught her arm and helped her down the stairs.

'What's your cabin number?'

'Eight.'

He propelled her along the corridor to her stateroom, and when they reached the door he took her handbag, extracted the key and unlocked it. Shaded lamps cast a pink glow over the turned-down bed and the violet chiffon nightdress draped over the pillow. Jane pushed it aside and fell back on the bed, not caring what she looked like or what happened to her.

Gradually she became aware of the whirring of fans and felt a cool breeze blowing against her face. The nausea had passed and she opened her eyes. At first glance she thought the cabin was empty, but as she turned her head she saw Stephen Drake by the dressing-table, looking at the books she had brought with her. At once Jane could have kicked herself; if there was one thing that gave away a person's character it was their choice of reading material. The man seemed to think so too, for he picked up a couple of books, looked at them and then put them down again.

'Proust, Ouspensky, Jane Austen,' he murmured. 'You're beginning to interest me, Miss Belton. A young girl with beauty, money and intelligence enough to *hide* her intelligence!'

'I never knew I made any attempt to hide it,' she said, and wondered whether she ought to close her eyes again and pretend to be ill.

'You haven't tried to hide it today,' he admitted, 'but I'm a newspaper proprietor, remember? I can recollect some pretty mad escapades you got up to. And none of them gave any indication that you read anything heavier than *Peg's*

Paper!'

'Oh, really?' she said weakly. 'What escapades are you thinking about?'

His eyes glittered dark. 'Well, there's the time you ran away from boarding school and went to Paris for two days, and there's your elopement with an Italian painter, and the time . . .'

His voice droned on, and Jane listened in horror to a recital of all she was supposed to have done, wondering why none of the stories had been in the press cuttings Frank Preston had given her to read. No wonder Stephen Drake found her books a contradiction of her character. Italian painter indeed! She moved on the bed and instantly he came over to her.

'Shall I ring for the stewardess to undress you?'

'There's no need. I don't think I'll bother getting undressed at all. I'll sleep the way I am.'

'Your dress isn't far short of a nightgown anyway,' he said humorously. 'Sometimes it beats me why women bother to wear anything at all! Particularly when what they wear is more revealing than nudity.'

'What a sharp tongue you've got,' she retorted. 'Now I've met you I'm quite sure you write some of the *Morning Star* editorials.'

'You've guessed my guilty secret! But in any case I'm glad to welcome you as a reader.'

She cursed herself for speaking without thinking. 'I read it because my – my father thinks I should read all the popular papers. He says it's important for me to keep in touch with the masses.'

'As you'll be inheriting Belton's Bakeries I can see the point! You know, you don't seem like a bread heiress to me. You're much more like a delicious French croissant!'

Jane burst out laughing, and he grinned. 'You seem much older than your age too,' he went on.

'That's because I'm an only child. And my father and I are very close together.'

49

'That's contradictory to what I've heard. Your father's got a reputation for being a very difficult man.'

'Only to strangers and business acquaintances.' Anxious to ward him off, she decided to toss the ball of conversation into his court.

'Anyway, you've no right to talk of contradictions, Mr. Drake! What about you? The first time we met you told me you wanted to be alone, yet you come on a cruise where you're bound to meet people!'

'I had to get out of the country quickly,' he said briefly, 'and this was the best boat. I'm under doctor's orders to forget business for a couple of months.'

'You don't look ill,' she ventured.

'Overwork doesn't always show. But I've been living on my nerves for the last few years.' He leaned against the wall in front of one of the lamps. It cast a pink glow over his skin, intensifying the tan and making him look more than ever like a pirate. 'As a matter of fact I intended asking you to have dinner with me tonight, but I took a sleeping pill this afternoon and woke up with a foul headache. Not the best of dinner companions.'

'I feel much better now,' she said brightly. 'I'll be able to get undressed after all.'

'In that case I'll go. Good night, child. Sweet dreams.'

The door closed behind him and Jane walked over to it and locked it. Turning, she saw her reflection in the mirror. Did she appear such a child to him? True, her blonde hair was awry and most of her make-up had smudged off on the pillow, but none the less there was allure in the depth of her eyes and passion in the full, red curve of her mouth. A picture of Claire Saunders, dark and imperious, came into her mind, and with it a picture of the unknown woman to whom Stephen Drake had been engaged. Strange that this woman should become synonymous in her mind with the débutante – probably because they both had the same unusual colouring. Had Stephen Drake noticed it yet? If not, then he would certainly become aware of it soon, for once the weather improved Claire would lose no time in setting her cap at him.

'That'll be a sight worth watching,' she thought, as she undressed and climbed between the sheets. 'But it would be a shame if he got hurt. He isn't really arrogant or unfriendly at all. He's just lonely – like so many men in his position. When you have to outbid and outpace other men you can't help being alone. What a good idea that would be for a series,' she mused sleepily. 'The loneliness of the long distance runner could so easily be changed to the loneliness of the big business tycoon.'

CHAPTER FOUR

JANE had no need to look out of the porthole the next morning to know that the weather had changed, for the sun was so brilliant it shone through the closed curtains, picking out her gold evening shoes on the carpet and glinting on the cut glass toilet accessories on the dressing-table.

She rang for breakfast, and while it was coming had a leisurely bath. Dressed in brief shorts and matching white silk shirt, she sat cross-legged on the bed, munching buttered croissants and remembering Stephen's description of her the night before.

When she stepped out on deck it was already crowded with sunbathers and many of them smiled at her as she walked by, looking for a vacant chair. One or two couples invited her to sit with them, but declining the offers she walked to the front of the deck where she had stood the previous day. There were no deck-chairs there either and she stood by the rail and looked out to sea. Below her was another deck and she leaned forward to look at it, surprised to catch a glimpse of a blue-tiled swimming-pool. Quickly she walked back the way she had come until she found a stairway and, reaching the lower deck, soon found herself by the side of the pool. Most of the younger set were here, and she stood by the side of the pool hoping a deck steward would come and find her a chair. The row in front of her was fully occupied and she moved a little away and waited.

'I don't like it,' a woman's voice said. 'I don't like it, and I'm afraid.'

'Don't be silly,' came the reply. 'You've nothing to be afraid of.'

Jane recognized the voice as belonging to Colin Waterman and she coughed loudly and took a step forward, anxious not to appear as if she were eavesdropping. Instantly a head appeared above the deck-chair and she looked into Colin's face.

'Hello,' he said in his precise, thin voice, and stood up. 'Come and sit here. Now that I've found you I'm not letting you out of my sight.'

Jane stepped round the side, surprised to see that Colin's companion was Claire Saunders.

'I don't want to take your chair,' she protested to him. 'I'm sure the steward—'

'Don't be silly. Sit down and I'll find myself another chair.'

'You needn't bother, Colin.' Claire stood up, her golden-skinned body clad in a lurex bathing-suit. A gold bracelet glinted on her wrist and a very narrow one on her ankle, adding to her exotic appearance. 'I want to go in for a swim and I'll go and sit on the other side where it's sunny and get warmed up first.'

With a cool nod at Jane she sauntered away, and Colin sat down in the vacated chair.

'I hope I didn't interrupt you,' Jane said.

'Not at all. In fact, I'm glad you did. When you got here Claire was bemoaning her spinsterhood. She's suddenly afraid that if she doesn't find a husband soon it'll be too late.'

Jane relaxed against the canvas. 'That's the sort of feeling a girl usually keeps to herself.'

'Then you can't know many girls of Claire's type. It's the sophisticated thing today to tell everyone your innermost feelings.'

'Then I'm not very sophisticated.'

'Thank goodness for that. It's one of the reasons I like you.' He leaned over, his face close to hers. 'And I do like you, Janey. I was sorry not to have seen you yesterday. But I felt too ill even to pick up the telephone. What did you do with yourself?'

'Talked to Stephen Drake – the man Claire noticed first night out.'

A look of amazement crossed Colin's bland face. 'So that's who he is. I wonder if Claire knows yet. Stephen Drake, eh?' He turned his head to where Claire was sunning herself on the opposite side of the pool. 'Well, talk of the devil,' he said softly. 'There he comes now.'

Jane followed his gaze and saw Stephen climbing the diving-board. His body, silhouetted against the blue sky, was the colour of mahogany, and even at a distance she could see the muscles rippling in his shoulders and out-stretched arms. Then he dived, hitting the water as smoothly as an arrow. Tired and overworked he might be, but it was more a mental than a physical illness, she thought, as she watched him surface and then strike out for the side in an effortless crawl.

Claire Saunders was watching the man too, and she stood up and walked over to the diving-board. All eyes were on her as she climbed gracefully to the top and stood there adjusting the straps of her suit. Her dive was as beautiful and controlled as that of the man, and when she rose to the top there was an appreciative murmur. As though unaware of it, she swam idly to the end of the pool, and watching, Jane was sure it was no coincidence that she should decide to climb out at the exact spot where Stephen Drake was sit-ting. Holding on to the side of the rail, she pulled herself up, half slipped back into the water and would have fallen had he not leaned forward and grabbed her. Jane was too far away to hear what was said, but she was intensely conscious that the man and woman were soon seated side by side, their feet dabbling the water, their bodies warmed by the sun.

'I might as well go and put my swimsuit on,' she said, and walked away, wishing she did not have to cross to the other side of the pool in order to reach the companionway. But it would look as if she were trying to avoid Claire and Stephen if she went in the other direction and, trying to appear as nonchalant as she could, she walked round the side of the pool. As she came closer to them her shadow fell across Stephen Drake's face and he turned and looked up.

54

'Good morning, Janey. Feeling better?'

'Yes, thank you.'

Claire said nothing, but the dark eyes watched her with an expression she could not fathom.

'Aren't you coming in for a swim?' he went on.

'I'm just going down to put on my suit.'

'Are you sure you're wise?' Claire laughed. 'Belinda said you hated the water.'

'Belinda?'

'Belinda Mitchell – my cousin. She was at school with you.'

'Oh, *Belinda*.' Jane forced herself to laugh. 'That was a long time ago. I've quite changed since then.'

'Only a couple of years,' Claire replied. 'And I'd be careful of the pool if I were you. There's no shallow end.'

Aware that she was being baited, Jane tilted her head and walked away. She was nearer the edge than she had realized and the ball of her foot slipped on the shiny tiles. Had there been anything to catch hold of she would not have lost her balance, but there was nothing within her grasp and she teetered precariously for a moment, her body swaying, her arms outstretched, before she toppled ignominiously into the water. Down to the bottom she went and came up spluttering, her hair clinging round her face. She was aware of laughter and she blinked the water out of her eyes and wished she were a million miles away. There was a splash beside her and firm hands gripped her shoulders.

'Don't worry,' Stephen Drake's voice said. 'A lot of people are afraid of the water.'

'I'm not afraid,' Jane spluttered, and tried to struggle away from him.

'Stop it,' he said, 'or you'll get yourself another unnecessary ducking. Lie still and I'll pull you in to the side.'

Jane did as she was told and a moment later was standing beside him on firm ground. Her shirt and shorts clung to her body and she was uncomfortably aware that the white silk outlined her far more than any swimming costume would have done. The man in front of her noticed it too, for his thin mouth curved in a smile and, reaching across to a vacant chair, he lifted off a towel and draped it over her shoulders.

Claire came up to them, her expression malicious, her voice sweet. 'Poor child, you did give yourself a ducking. I wish I'd had my movie camera. You looked screamingly funny!'

'I'm sure I did.' Jane coughed up some more water, and Claire grinned openly.

'It serves you right for saying you could swim. I knew Belinda wasn't lying.'

'Blow Belinda,' Jane said, and Stephen Drake chuckled.

'*I'll* teach you to swim if you like,' he said. 'It's all a matter of confidence. Once you've got over your initial fear I'm sure you'll be fine.'

'It's very kind of you,' she said, and wondered whether it would be difficult to pretend to be inexpert at a sport at which she excelled. What luck she had had the presence of mind not to go into a speedy crawl when she had surfaced in the bath! 'I don't think I'll go swimming any more today,' she continued. 'But I'll take you up on your offer tomorrow.'

'We dock at Cannes in the morning,' Claire intervened.

'In that case we'll postpone our lesson till the day after.' Stephen Drake touched Jane's arm. 'Perhaps you'll let me show you the sights instead, if you're not already going ashore with someone?'

Jane stood perfectly still, surprised at the unexpectedness of his invitation. Claire was surprised too, for though she had the presence of mind not to show it on her face, her body had grown rigid.

'No, I'm not going with anyone,' Jane said breathlessly. 'I'd like to go with you very much.'

'Good.' He patted her shoulder. 'Now go and change into

some dry things.'

Happily Jane sped away, and while rubbing herself dry in her stateroom thought what an extraordinary man he was: casual and stand-offish one moment, irrationally charming the next. One thing was certain: whatever tomorrow brought it would not be boredom.

'Fancy me going out with the great Stephen Drake! If only Frank Preston were here to see it.'

Thoughts of Frank Preston made her realize that as far as her features editor was concerned she was on the trip for one purpose only: to cable back news. And though she would have enjoyed relaxing by the pool, as soon as she had changed into a play-suit and rubbed her hair dry, she returned to the deck and wandered slowly past the sunbathers. This time she did not refuse when she was asked to join some of them, and the rest of the day passed in chit-chat with different people.

During the afternoon, while Greg Pearson, Ace Films' number one heart-throb, was showing her the correct way to do the cha-cha, Stephen Drake and Claire Saunders strolled past and stopped to watch, Claire's expression one of patronizing amusement. 'Strange that she should make me feel so naïve,' Jane thought crossly. 'And there's no doubt she's doing it deliberately.' The knowledge that it *was* deliberate was heart-warming since it meant Claire feared her. Yet why should she fear her? Because of Colin Waterman? Jane dismissed this at once, since Claire had known Colin for years and had presumably had her chance with him. No, the answer was Stephen Drake. Claire was setting out to attract him and was determined to minimize any competition she might encounter. 'Fancy me, lowly little Jane Berry, being competition for a rich young socialite!'

The irony of the situation did not please her and she wished she could have met Stephen without any subterfuge or lies. It was suddenly important that he should not think badly of her, and though she knew she could justify her actions on the grounds that she was doing it for his own paper, from her knowledge of the man she knew he would not easily forgive anyone who made a fool of him.

'Hey, Janey!' Greg Pearson's drawling voice with its pseudo-American accent broke into her thoughts. 'We're supposed to be doing the cha-cha, remember, and you're a million miles away.'

'Sorry, Greg, I was just thinking.'

'A beautiful girl like you has no business to think!' Greg pulled her close. 'Now come on, baby, give with the hips!'

By the end of the day Jane had culled enough material to be able to return to her cabin and write a long article. With so many celebrities on board no reporter worthy of the name could have failed to concoct a dozen human interest stories, but she had had to be careful how she had gathered her material, for questions that came naturally from a reporter were apt, unless carefully worded, to sound impertinent from a girl ostensibly indulging in social conversation.

It said much for her ability that she was able to extract her information without exciting suspicion, and her pen flew over the paper as she turned all that she had learned into paragraphs which she knew would be lapped up by the readers of the *Morning Star*.

So intent was she on writing that she did not hear the dinner bell, and by the time she looked up from her pad it was nearly nine-thirty. Her head was aching and, unable to face the prospect of changing, she ordered a light snack to be brought to her cabin. The *Cambrian* would be docking at Cannes at nine the next morning and she wanted to be fresh for the forthcoming day.

When the yacht dropped anchor outside Cannes Harbour the sky was already a fierce blue, its colour echoed in deeper tones in the water. The harbour itself was filled with yachts bobbing and tossing in the breeze, and though from this distance she could not distinguish the Croisette itself, she was able to make out the gaily coloured awnings of the restaurants that lined the quayside and the twin towers of the Carlton Hotel further along the promenade. Even from this distance there was a magic quality about her first sight of the Côte D'Azur, a quality enhanced by the crispness of the air and the muted colours of the grey-green hills that receded into the distance.

'It's a lovely sight, isn't it?' a voice said behind her, and she swung round to see her escort. Once more he was wearing navy slacks, but his shirt this time was white silk and emphasized the blackness of his hair. 'I suppose you've seen it many times before?'

'As a matter of fact I haven't. I've been to Paris and the Normandy coast, but never as far south as this.'

'Then I look forward to showing you a bit of the real France hidden away behind the glamour.'

In the distance they heard the chugging of an outboard motor, and he leaned over the rail. 'We'll be able to embark in a minute. They've already lowered the gangplank.'

'Is everyone going ashore?'

'I should think so, if only to buy perfume! The richer the people the bigger their desire to find bargains.'

Jane longed to ask him where Claire was, but as she descended the gangplank she glimpsed the girl walking along the deck with Colin. There was a sullen expression on her face and Colin too seemed ill at ease. Poor man! He was no doubt getting the benefit of Claire's temper!

But soon all thoughts of Colin and Claire were forgotten as she took her place in the small boat and felt the salt spray beating against her skin.

'I should have warned you to bring a scarf,' the man at her side said. 'Sea water will ruin your hair set.'

'How knowledgeable you are about women!' The laughter in her voice died as she felt him stiffen beside her, and realized that his schooling must have come from the woman to whom he had been engaged.

Within a few moments they were on shore and Jane was astonished to see the Croisette packed with cars, most of them gleaming roadsters and all seemingly occupied by bronzed, handsome men, and women who resembled either

Brigitte Bardot or Sophia Loren. She was glad she was wearing one of Janey's more sophisticated outfits, a pleated dress of blue shantung that almost matched the colour of her eyes. The bodice was cut lower than she would normally have worn, and she made a conscious effort to keep her shoulders well back. One could show almost everything in a bikini without attracting a second glance, yet a bodice cut an inch too low took on an extraordinarily provocative appearance.

'Horse or horse-power?' Stephen Drake asked as he led her across the quay to the *fiacres* and cabs lining up for their first customers.

'Horse, please.' Seeing him smile, she said defensively: 'I suppose you think I'm silly?'

'Young, but not silly.' Holding out his hand, he helped her up into the rickety carriage.

It was the first time Jane had ever ridden in a *fiacre*, and though the horse moved slowly the carriage shook from side to side, giving the impression of great speed and making her cling breathlessly to the sides.

'Relax,' her escort said. 'I promise you'll come to no harm!' He pulled her back against him and she was intensely conscious of his thigh pressing against hers. 'That's better,' he said and, putting his arm round the top of the seat, let his hand rest lightly on her shoulder. 'These horses are very sure-footed and you've nothing to worry about.'

'I'm not worried. I just feel as if I'm being put through a blender.'

He laughed. 'What a funny kid you are. You have the strangest expressions.'

'I wish you wouldn't call me a kid, Mr. Drake.'

'The name's Stephen. And I'm sorry if I sounded fatherly. But you must blame your blonde hair. It makes you look so young.'

'Blondes are supposed to look sophisticated.

'Not when their hair curls up at the ends like ducks' tails.'

60

At the teasing in his voice she felt as though a hand were pressing against her throat making it difficult to breathe. More aware of his glance than ever, she turned her head away and concentrated on the scenery. The palm-lined Croisette would have been beautiful had it not been for the preponderance of cars, but even so she could appreciate the luxury of the hotels set back from the road, many of them with their own terraces dotted with small tables and gaily coloured umbrellas. White-coated waiters were already serving aperitifs, and holiday-makers were strolling down to the narrow stretch of sand covered from end to end with deck-chairs and mattresses and sunshades.

Presently the *fiacre* left the main road and took an uphill path between stretches of pine wood. The road became steeper as they climbed, and after about half an hour the driver reined in his horse and spoke volubly to Stephen. His accent was too thick for Jane to follow, but she was aware of many gesticulations towards the animal between the shafts.

'Is anything wrong?' she asked.

'He says it's too steep for the horse,' Stephen answered. 'I was a fool not to have realized it myself.'

'What a pity he didn't tell us before.'

'I expect he didn't want to lose the fare.' Suddenly he leaned over the side of the carriage and waved his arm. A small car screeched to a stop and he jumped down on to the road and held out his hand to Jane. 'We can take a taxi the rest of the way. At least you've had your buggy ride.'

Soon they were driving along the Grande Corniche with Cannes far below them and olive groves ahead. For more than an hour they drove along the winding road, negotiating the hairpin bends with a turn of speed that petrified her. Stephen did not even appear to notice and sat smoking a cigarette in a corner of the car. Soon they turned off from the main highway, and as they drove deeper into the heart of Provence the air grew heavier and warmer. They drove slowly through many villages, and Jane was delighted by the beautiful play of shadows on the cobbled roads and the tall trees that formed a green canopy high above their heads.

They stopped for a drink at a small bistro and sat at a table on the pavement watching the passers-by – plump, dark-skinned women doing their shopping and small knots of men indulging in a never-ending conversation, while children played marbles around a small fountain.

'I'm always promising myself I'll tour Provence, village by village,' Stephen said as he sipped his Dubonnet and lit another cigarette. 'I think this is the real France. Here you can feel its heart beat. Not at all like the phoney glamour of Cannes or Nice. Still, maybe you'd have preferred to stay there? I'm afraid I took it for granted you'd like something quiet.'

'I do. It's a pleasure to get away from people. Besides, when you're in Cannes you could just as easily be in Bournemouth – except for the difference in food and language! But here—' she waved her arm, indicating a woman carrying a French loaf a yard long and shouting at a swarthy-skinned child leading a donkey by the reins – 'here it's unmistakably different.'

He nodded and, dropping some coins on the table, stood up. 'Come on, Janey. We've still got a way to go.'

'Where are you taking me?'

'To a place I know where they serve the best lunch on the coast. It's not as pretentious as La Mer Terrasse or La Bonne Auberge, but the food's even better.'

They drove for another half hour, climbing high into the hills before finally stopping at a low-storeyed villa, its walls painted pink, the doors and windows heavily covered with bougainvillea.

An elderly man in a white jacket greeted Stephen with an exclamation of pleasure and led him through a flat-tiled hall to a large terrace set with tables and tall columns around which twined dark green leaves. The view that met Jane's eyes was breathtakingly beautiful. Endless groves of olive trees stretched for miles and beyond them in the hazy distance shimmered the sea. There was no sound of cars to spoil the peace, only the chirping of crickets and the buzzing of the cicadas.

'Have you any preference as to what you'd like to eat?' Stephen asked as they sat at a table on the edge of the terrace, 'or will you leave it me?'

Knowing that he hoped she would do just this, Jane nodded and listened with amusement as he proceeded to order. It was not an order quickly given nor lightly accepted, for he and the *patron* had lengthy discussions over every item. Jane was able to follow this conversation, but could not make head or tail of the dishes eventually decided upon, and said as much when they were left alone.

'Theirs not to reason why,' Stephen replied. 'But of course if you'd like steak and two veg . . .'

She laughed and leaned back in her chair. 'It's glorious here. We seem miles from civilization.'

'This *is* civilization. The life that's led down below—' he waved his arm '—isn't life at all. It's a meaningless round of activity, and the people who indulge in it are like mice on a wheel, going round and round and never getting anywhere.'

'You're on the wheel too,' she reminded him. 'And your wheel is bigger and faster than anyone else's!'

'I know. Sometimes I've a notion to give it all up and live on an island miles away from anyone.'

'What stops you?'

He did not answer, but his expression was so bleak that she leaned forward and touched his arm. 'You're depressed because you're tired, Stephen. There's been too much output in the last few years and not enough input. A month of rest will give you the energy to go on.'

'Go on,' he said dully. 'Go on to where and to what? And for whom?'

'The last question is the most important,' she said softly. 'It's for *whom* that matters to you most. If you had someone for whom you wanted to work, your whole life would take on meaning. It isn't empty because you have to work, it's empty because you don't love. That's why you're lonely, too.'

'How do you know I'm lonely?'

'We're all lonely without love.'

'What about your great saints? Or your priests? What love did they have?'

'Love of God. It doesn't matter what it's love *of*.' She smiled. 'As long as it's not love of self.'

He was a long time replying, and when he did his answer was surprising.

'I've never talked to a woman the way I've talked to you. It's as if I've known you all my life. I thought at first it was because we were on a ship and ships do strange things to people. But we're on firm ground now and the feeling is still the same.' He smiled slightly. 'Somehow I can't think of you as Cedric Belton's daughter. You're not an heiress type, Janey. In fact, you're not even a Janey! It's a ridiculous name and it doesn't suit you.'

'I agree with you. I'd much rather you called me Jane.'

'Jane. That's much better. Yes, you are a Jane. Reserved and warm.'

Jane closed her eyes, listening not so much to what he said as to the way he said it. To have him call her by her own name made her feel less of an impostor, and once more she knew a longing to reveal her identity. In the normal way she— Abruptly she opened her eyes and brought herself back to reality. In the normal way the nearest she could have got to Stephen Drake was a name on a staff list!

At that moment the *patron* arrived with the first of many delicious courses, and she forgot the past and the future and savoured only the present. And what a mouth-watering present it was: vine leaves stuffed with rice and olives, *moules farcies à la Provençale* – mussels covered with egg yolks and butter and golden breadcrumbs – and *côtes de volaille* – chicken breasts with smoked ham and *foie gras* fried in butter, the meal ending with *omelette soufflée*, a golden ball of lightness flavoured with Grand Marnier and cognac.

'I don't think I'll ever be able to eat again,' she said as she spooned up the last delicious mouthful.

'I'm glad you thought it worth the drive!'

'Oh, I do.'

Yet it was not so much the food she appreciated as the hours she had been able to spend alone with Stephen. She had expected him to have a keen mind and to be highly intelligent. But she had been unprepared for his sense of humour, his sympathetic outlook and warm understanding of many problems.

It was only as they strolled from the terrace and began to walk through the woods below that he expressed the same surprise in her.

'I assume you've led a sheltered existence,' he said, 'yet you seem extremely knowledgeable about a great many things.' He caught her arm as she stumbled over the root of a tree. 'Where did you learn so much about life? I assume it wasn't from your school!'

'It certainly wasn't,' she laughed, and wondered what he would say if he knew that he himself had paid for much of her experience. She remembered the tedious weeks she had spent in Glasgow, culling information for a series of articles, and the days she had spent sitting on hard benches in dreary courts as the washed-out dregs of humanity had shambled through them. It was difficult to retain one's idealism in such circumstances, difficult to keep up the pretence of being naïve and uncaring of the world. Yet so many reporters did stop caring, became cynical and weary, regarded other people's tragedies as their own good stories.

'Come back, Jane.' Stephen's voice was teasing. 'You've a strange habit of mentally disappearing.'

'I'm sorry.' She walked on more quickly, nervous of his closeness and of her own reaction to it.

The air was cool in the wood and the lemon gloom was occasionally broken by a slanting ray of sunlight. The ground beneath her feet was slippery with pine needles, but Stephen's hand was always ready to help her. Gradually the trees began to thin out until they reached an open space at the bottom of the hill. Here the grass was dry and yellowing, and she sank down on it. He sprawled beside her, his lean face upturned to the sun, his hands clasped beneath his head.

'I'd forgotten how beautiful it was,' he said. 'It's so long since I've been here.'

'Sometimes it isn't good to come back.'

He was silent for a moment as though considering her statement. 'It's been even better this time,' he said at last. 'When I was here before I was alone.'

Jane's cheeks burned and she turned her head away, hoping he had not noticed. How stupid of her to blush like a schoolgirl because a man paid her a compliment! The silence between them lengthened, became so heavy with unspoken thoughts that she was compelled to break it.

'You're braver than I am, Stephen. I've always thought it a mistake to retrace one's steps.'

He smiled. 'It isn't like you to be cynical.'

'I'm not cynical,' she protested. 'Only I think we either tend to glamorize the past or else give it an intensity it never had. Return to a place that once gave you happiness and you're pretty sure to find it deadly. Meet someone you used to love and you're pretty sure to . . .' Her voice trailed away and she looked at her hands, wishing she could draw back the words. But words once said could never be unspoken, could rarely be forgotten.

'I wonder if you're right.' His voice was almost inaudible. 'I wish to God I could find out.'

'Maybe you – you'll meet her.'

'Meet whom?' he asked sharply.

'Georgina.' Jane waited for him to explode, but he merely sighed.

'I'll tell you if I do. I promise you that.' He jumped to his feet. 'Come on, child, we've a long drive ahead of us and I wouldn't like us to miss the boat.'

'It would be terrible for my reputation,' she giggled.

'I didn't think you young things worried about that. I do, but then I'm old-fashioned.'

'When men say they're old-fashioned they generally mean they have one standard for themselves and another standard for their womenfolk!'

The thick black eyebrows lifted in surprise. 'And what exactly does that mean?'

'Merely that men don't mind living it up themselves, but expect the woman they marry to have lived the life of a nun.'

He nodded. 'You're right, of course. The act of love doesn't mean to a man what it does to a woman. For him it's a necessary physical outlet, but for her it means the accepting of life itself.' They walked in silence for a few yards. 'One's attitude to women,' he went on quietly, 'is often governed by one's upbringing and childhood. My mother was a proud woman and suffered a great deal from my father. He didn't know the meaning of faithfulness, and I grew up determined never to treat any woman the way he treated her. If I marry I want my wife to regard me with as much respect as I'd want to regard *her*.'

'I understand,' she said gently and, turning, smiled at him. The sun was behind her head, turning her hair into a nimbus of gold and shadowing her blue eyes so that they glowed dark as sapphires. She heard him catch his breath and stare at her intently.

'You look so innocent, Jane. I find it hard to believe that . . .'

His voice trailed away, and she tilted her head inquiringly.

'Find it hard to believe what?'

'Nothing,' he said abruptly, and quickening his pace led the way to the car.

CHAPTER FIVE

It was late afternoon when they reached Cannes again and drove slowly through the crowded streets towards the harbour.

'Do you want to go straight back on board,' Stephen asked, 'or would you like to stroll along the Croisette?'

'A stroll, please.'

He signalled the driver to stop, and while he paid him off, Jane jumped out and walked across the promenade to look at the beach.

'You've forgotten your bag,' Stephen called after her, and held it out, his fingers pressing against its bulky sides. The rustle of paper was audible and he smiled. 'Hm, you must be writing a long letter to someone.'

Jane's heart thumped. Her copy to the *Morning Star*! How awful if the bag had opened and he had seen the closely written sheets of paper. She almost snatched the bag from him and tucked it under her arm. 'I must find a post office. I've some cards to send off.'

'Why don't you give them to the Purser? Foreign post offices are the devil.'

'I'll feel safer if I post them myself.'

'Very well. We'll go and find a post office and you can make yourself happy buying stamps.'

He guided her over the road, no mean feat considering the speed and number of the cars dashing past, and they walked up one of the turnings towards the town. Her mind was filled with the problem of how she could go into the post office alone and send off her copy to Frank Preston, and she looked up with a start as Stephen indicated a large building and began to walk up the steps.

'You needn't come in,' she said quickly.

'I might as well get some stamps for myself.'

'No, honestly, I won't be a moment.' She pulled her arm out of his grasp and dashed up the rest of the stairs, disappearing into the building like a rabbit to its hole.

Once inside she glanced fearfully behind to make sure he had not followed and, finding herself on her own, hurried to the nearest counter. With trembling hands she took out the bulky envelope and slid it over to the assistant, her fear not abating until she saw the envelope disappear into one of the chutes.

When she went outside again Stephen was leaning against the wall, his face unsmiling. Silently they returned to the Croisette and he set off in the direction of the harbour.

'We might as well get back,' he muttered. 'I feel tired.'

Gone was the ease between them, and in its place was a stiff formality. Try as she would she could see no reason why he should be so annoyed because she had wanted to go into the post office alone. Taken at its face value it was simply a desire not to have him wait in a stuffy atmosphere while she did some necessary chores. He had no right to stride along beside her with such an angry scowl. It was an unfortunate end to what had otherwise been a happy day, and unaccustomed tears pricked her eyes. 'Fancy crying over a thing like this,' she thought angrily, and blinked her lids. No doubt it was because she was miles away from home, in a foreign country surrounded by strangers. If only she could be herself, if only there was no need for pretence! She could not bear to have Stephen angry with her, and she caught his arm.

'Stephen, I'm sorry. I didn't think you wanted to wait inside the post office for me. I know you thought me childish not giving my letters to the Purser, and I wanted to be as quick as I could.'

He looked at her without expression. 'There's no need to apologize. If you had letters to post that you didn't want me to see . . .'

'Why should you think that?'

'It seemed obvious. Apart from which you have a repu-

69

tation for unwise romantic entanglements.'

She raised her eyes and looked at him steadily. 'The letter *was* to a man, but he's middle-aged and devoted to his wife and four children. I swear that's true.'

He said nothing and continued to walk, but Jane saw that the scowl was no longer on his face, although it still held an expression she could not fathom. Only when they were in a little boat chugging across the water to the *Cambrian* did she understand fully what else was in his mind.

'All those stories about you,' he said abruptly. 'For a young girl you've led a pretty hectic life.'

'Newspaper stories,' she answered, crossing her fingers surreptitiously.

'There must have been *some* truth in them.' He groped in his pocket for a cigarette. 'What about the time you eloped with that Italian painter?'

Jane caught her breath and stared at the sea as if she could find her answer on the waves. 'All girls get crushes on someone. It was just bad luck that some – some horrible reporter got hold of it and blew it up into a seven-day wonder.' She swung round and looked at him, determined to make him see she was telling the truth. 'It meant absolutely nothing to me. Why, he never even kissed me!'

Without realizing it, by the very ingenuousness of her remark she had convinced Stephen she was speaking the truth. He threw back his head and laughed.

'That's a Janey remark,' he said as he recovered his composure. 'But I'm glad you're Jane now.'

They were the last passengers to board the ship and as the motor-boat sped back to the shore they heard the anchor being wound up.

'It's been a wonderful day,' she said happily, and held out her hand to him. 'The first time I saw you, you were so stand-offish I never expected us to be spending the whole day together like this.'

'I'd no intention of it either,' he said. 'But I've enjoyed every moment. I'll see you later this evening.'

70

Although tired from her day's excursion, Jane was too excited to rest and spent the intervening hour before changing for dinner carefully examining the clothes in her wardrobe. On close inspection they were breathtakingly beautiful, though a couple of them were not to her particular taste. What should she wear tonight?

Staring at herself some time later, she could not hold back an exclamation of pleasure. A blue silk cat-suit outlined her slim figure. Her soft blonde hair was piled high on her head, held in place with a jewelled comb. The tips of her ears glowed pink with excitement and she wished momentarily that she could wear the pearl earrings and necklace she had seen among Janey's jewellery. But better not to tempt fate, she decided, and picking up her handbag, went out.

She was half-way down the corridor when Claire Saunders, in black, came out of her cabin, and Jane stopped and smiled at her, ignoring a wave of antagonism so strong that it was almost tangible.

'Well, well,' Claire drawled. '*You've* grown up fast!'

'It's just a different hair-style,' Jane replied. 'I was tired of having it flap around my face.'

'It takes more than upswept hair to convince a man you're not a child.'

Jane ignored this and they began to walk towards the dining-room. Beside Claire she felt small and unimportant, and though she knew it was an inferiority complex born of lack of confidence and in no way connected with her outward appearance, she could not overcome it. The assurance that came with social background and wealth could not be acquired merely by the donning of expensive clothes, and the knowledge depressed her, making her realize the difficulties of stepping from one world to another.

They descended the stairs and ahead were the shining glass doors leading to the dining-room. Claire paused and lifted her foot to inspect one of her shoes.

'Did you enjoy your day with Stephen?' she asked casually.

'Very much. We lunched at a restaurant in the hills and drove round the countryside.'

'How sweet of Stephen to bother. It must have been an awful bore for him.'

'I don't think so,' Jane said defensively. 'He suggested it himself.'

'That just goes to show how sweet he is,' Claire repeated. 'Originally we were going to spend the day at Cap Ferrat. Some friends of mine have a villa there.' She put her foot to the ground, but remained motionless. 'When you fell into the pool yesterday he felt so sorry for you that on the spur of the moment he asked you out. Naturally I told him I didn't mind. I took Colin to the villa instead and . . .'

Claire continued to talk, but Jane did not hear a word, anger making her heart pound so violently that she was deaf to all that went on around her. Indeed she was not even conscious of walking into the dining-room or taking her place at the table. So Stephen had asked her to spend the day with him merely out of kindness. Did he think she was a child who had to be placated? And what arrogance to assume *he* had the right to do the placating!

Fury took away her appetite and she picked at her food, gulping down her wine with unusual recklessness. Gradually the alcohol dulled her anger and by the time she was served her sweet she was able to take part in the conversation around her. The Pendleburys had spent the day at the Carlton Hotel with a short trip to Juan les Pins to buy – Lady Pendlebury assured her – 'the most divine sports clothes in the world'. Colin had gone with Claire to her friends' villa and painful red sunburn testified to a day by the swimming-pool.

'I hope you'll let *me* take you out on the next excursion,' he said. 'I'd no idea Drake was going to ask you.'

'Neither had I,' Jane replied truthfully.

'Well, I don't intend to let him monopolize you any more. There's dancing in the ballroom tonight and I'd like you to be my partner.'

'You can't monopolize the prettiest girl aboard,' a drawling voice said, and Jane and Colin turned to see Greg Pearson smiling at them. In a frilled white shirt and a pale blue dinner jacket he looked every massaged inch a film star.

'Considering I spent the best part of an hour teaching Janey to cha-cha,' he went on, 'the least she can do in return is to dance it with me tonight!'

'I'll dance with anyone who asks me,' she said lightly. 'I don't think people should monopolize each other on a ship. After all, that's the whole purpose of a cruise, isn't it – that everyone should get together.' She pushed back her chair. 'I must go upstairs. It's so terribly hot in here.'

'It's the wine you've been drinking,' Colin said humorously. 'You'd better not go straight out into the air or you'll fall flat on your face!'

Jane tossed her head, but as she moved away from the table the floor wavered beneath her and she was glad of Colin's steadying hand at her elbow.

'See what I mean?' he whispered. 'Now you hold on to me and I'll get you out of here in the perpendicular. But one peep out of you about not dancing with me and I'll leave you flat!'

She giggled and clung to his arm as they walked the length of the room. Only as they reached the door did she see Stephen approaching it, and as they came close he turned to her and smiled. She refused to meet his gaze and continued to talk animatedly to Colin, fiercely glad of the look of surprise that crossed Stephen's face as she passed him.

The orchestra was already playing in the ballroom.

'Come on,' Colin said, 'it's a pity to waste the whole evening!' Pulling her on the floor, he began to dance.

Jane's head was almost on a level with his and she was able to look directly into his face. Seen at such proximity he did not look as young as she had first taken him to be, and she saw that the fairness of his hair was liberally sprinkled with silver. There were lines around his eyes and mouth and a hardness in his expression that one did not notice when looking at him from any distance. It was as if the very blondness and pinkness of him disguised his character, and she gave herself another warning not to relax too much in his presence. Although she had no doubt that he would keep her secret, she did not intend to tempt fate and end up the way Hawton had done. She shivered at the thought and Colin gave her a little shake.

'Hey there, Janey, is anything worrying you?'

She shook her head. 'I guess it isn't good for a girl to come on a cruise alone. She needs someone to talk to.'

'You can talk to me.'

'That's not what I mean.'

'Well, if you're looking for a female confidante don't go to Claire. She was furious at the way you snaffled Drake today.'

'I know. She told me.'

'Did she now?' Colin's eyebrows, so fair that they were barely noticeable, drew together in a frown. 'I wouldn't take much notice of what she says, Janey. She can be damned spiteful when she wants to be.'

Jane did not reply, but hearing her sigh Colin squeezed her waist and swirled off into a series of intricate steps that required all her concentration.

It was not until much later that she noticed Stephen and Claire. They were sitting with a group of middle-aged people, the men all smoking cigars, the women ablaze with jewellery. At the centre was a plump man with a mass of white hair and small but gesticulating arms, whom Jane at once guessed to be Dinky Howard. Whatever story he was telling was exceedingly entertaining, for the company around him seemed amused, and Jane's anger returned as she saw Stephen throw back his head and join in the laughter. Even as she watched he held out his hand to Claire, leading her on to the floor as the orchestra went into the strains of a tango.

They were a striking-looking couple, both tall and dark and both moving with grace. Whatever she had expected him to be Jane had not expected him to be an excellent dancer, believing he would find such a pastime a waste of effort. But an excellent dancer he certainly was, and all eyes were on him and the Spanish-looking beauty in his arms. As the music finished there was a spatter of applause and Claire's head lifted proudly, her hand remaining possessively on his shoulder.

But her look of pleasure faded as the band swung into a Paul Jones and within a moment Sir Brian Pendlebury had commandeered her, leaving Stephen to dance with a short fat woman in mauve damask.

'We can't sit this one out,' Greg Pearson said, and pulled Jane to her feet.

'But it's a Paul Jones,' she protested. 'We won't be able to—'

Her words were cut off as another pair of arms clasped her and she found herself being whirled from one man to another. The music increased in tempo and, pleased at the number of dancers thronging the floor, Dinky Howard signalled the band to keep the Paul Jones going. Jane looked longingly around for the safety of Colin's presence, but he was manfully propelling the mauve damask, and she could not help smiling at the look of painful determination on his face.

The music changed again and one more pair of arms claimed her. Without even raising her head she knew from the throbbing of her body who it was. She missed a step and stumbled and the arms tightened.

'So much dancing at such a late hour for such a little girl,' a deep voice said. 'Why is Jane behaving like Janey to-night?'

She raised her head and looked into Stephen's face. 'The two are not indivisible. I'm Jane *and* Janey.'

'Little Miss Muffet and Mata Hari,' he chuckled. 'What's the matter, Jane, have I offended you?'

'Of course not. Why do you ask?'

'Because of the way you snubbed me earlier this evening.'

'I didn't see you.'

'Rubbish. If I—'

He stopped as the music changed again and, seeing another man come purposefully towards them, gripped her arm and pulled her through the open glass door directly behind him. Still not letting her go, he propelled her along the deck until the ballroom was out of sight and the orchestra merely a throb of sound on the air.

'What a relief to get into the quiet,' he said, and still not releasing her, leaned against the rail.

More than ever she was aware of his nearness and of the warmth that emanated from him, the sharp smell of his shaving lotion blending with the aroma of cigar. But beneath it was the vibrant smell of the man himself, the warmth of skin and touch that made her long to rest her body against his. 'What price emancipation for women now?' she thought desperately. One glance from the right man, one touch and all one's desire for freedom was forgotten in the longing to be conquered and taken!

She tried to pull her hand away from his, but the fluttering of her fingers only made him hold them more tightly.

'No, you don't,' he said. 'You're not going to run away from me just yet. I want an answer to the question I asked you earlier.'

'What question?'

'Why you suddenly froze up on me.'

She debated whether to tell him the truth and decided against it. If he learned the reason for her anger it would not take him long to deduce why she should be so hurt. And she could not bear him to know the truth. Could not bear him to know that she loved him. There, it was out! At last she admitted consciously what she had subconsciously been aware of ever since she had first spoken to him. She loved him. She trembled so violently that she leaned against the rail to steady herself, shivering at its coldness against her arms. How could she love a man she hardly knew? A man so far out of her reach that he might as well be on another

76

planet?

'Well, Jane?' he said into her ear. 'You still haven't answered my question.'

'There's nothing – nothing to answer. I'm sorry you should have misjudged my attitude. I was just trying to let you know that it wasn't – it wasn't necessary for you to continue being nice to me.'

'But I like being nice to you, whether you think it's necessary or not.'

She did not say anything and continued to look out at the dark sea, the tips of the waves silvered by moonlight. Behind her he moved and the breeze that was gently touching her shoulders was blotted out by the heavier touch of his hands. She shivered and turning protestingly came face to face with him. How different he looked now, his eyes narrow slits, his sunken cheeks giving him a demoniac appearance and his mouth . . . She had no chance to look at his mouth, for it was suddenly pressed down on hers. There was no chance to draw back, no chance to resist; and she was overcome by an emotion she had never experienced before, half fear, half ecstasy and wholly desirous of surrender.

Again and again he kissed her, until her senses cried out that unless she could stop him, it would be too late. With all her strength she pushed against him and he released her so abruptly that she staggered back against the rail.

'I'm sorry,' he said thickly. 'I shouldn't have done that. It's the ship . . . I told you it destroyed one's barriers, didn't I?'

Without another word he strode across the deck and disappeared down one of the companionways, leaving Jane alone with the shadows and the sea and her own turbulent thoughts.

CHAPTER SIX

In the morning Jane found her behaviour of the night before inexplicable. Sunlight made her fears ridiculous, and she was angry that she had not told Stephen all that Claire had said. Her belief that he would guess what she felt for him was merely the outcome of her own knowledge and had nothing whatever to do with reality. Indeed, he was far more likely to suspect her emotions if she were to go on behaving in this childish way. The only possible solution was to put up a sophisticated front, to let him see that she did not care what his reason was for asking her to spend the day in Cannes with him.

As soon as she had finished breakfast she went on deck and, ignoring the bustle around the swimming pool, settled herself in a deck-chair in the lee of a dinghy which swung in davits above her head and made an ideal shady spot.

Hardly had she opened her magazine and started to read than a shadow fell across the page and Colin squatted on the deck beside her.

'You know I'm keeping a place for you by the pool,' he said reproachfully. 'You've no right to hide yourself away like this.'

She laughed. 'If I intended to hide I can assure you I'd do it more successfully. I just don't fancy sitting in the blazing sun.'

He grunted and looked at her in such open admiration that she was uncomfortably aware of the briefness of her pink bikini.

'When you blush you look like a strawberry,' he grinned, and leaned closer. 'I like the way you've framed your hair with that white bandage.'

Embarrassment was forgotten in amusement. 'It's not a bandage, it's a bandeau. When I put oil on my face it stops my hair getting greasy.'

'You don't need any oil, you're a lovely sherry colour already. It's unusual for a blonde to tan the way you do.'

'What compliments, Colin! I can see why you've got your reputation.'

'I hope you don't believe all you've read about me in the papers. I've settled down considerably in the last few years.'

'Not enough to be caught, though. You're still a matrimonial catch.'

He squinted at her in the sunlight. 'I'm glad you think so. You're quite a catch yourself.' He placed his hand on her arm and she noted with surprise how beautifully shaped it was, more like a girl's than a man's, with tapering fingers and filbert nails.

Footsteps sounded on the deck and she tried to draw her arm away, but he refused to let go, only relaxing his grip as Claire's drawling voice came across to them.

'I thought I'd find you here, Colin. Have you forgotten we're in a deck quoits competition?'

He got to his feet unconcernedly. 'I'm afraid I had. Sorry, Claire.'

'If you don't want to play I'll find another partner.'

'Don't be silly. Of course I'll play.'

With a smile at Jane he allowed Claire to lead him away, and she watched them go, her amusement tinged by puzzlement. For someone who professed herself to be uninterested in Colin, Claire was surprisingly possessive of him, but perhaps she was the sort of girl who was possessive of any man the moment another woman looked at him?

'She's welcome to *all* the men on board,' Jane thought irritably, and concentrated on her magazine again.

Even in the shade it was warm, and her hair clung to the back of her neck in damp curls. The sea was as smooth as satin, and the gentle movement of the ship caused no breeze. The print blurred before her eyes and she closed them and leaned her head back. The splash of water in the pool, the sound of laughter and the occasional call of a bird high in the sky magnified itself in her ears and then receded as she fell asleep.

She awoke with a start, conscious of someone watching her and, tilting her head, saw Stephen. Quickly she sat up.

'You startled me!' she exclaimed.

'I'm sorry. I was going to creep away when you woke up.'

'How long have you been here?'

'Only a moment. Why?'

'I hate being watched when I'm asleep. It's – it's embarrassing.'

He laughed, his teeth gleaming white in his dark face. 'You've no need to feel embarrassed. You look far prettier asleep than most people do when they're awake.'

He pulled up another chair and stretched out on it. 'I'm glad you're awake, though, because I want to apologize for my behaviour last night.'

'There's no need. In fact, I was the one who behaved stupidly.'

He shook his head. 'I shouldn't have kissed you the way I did. But you looked so sophisticated and beautiful that I forgot you're only a child.'

'I'm not a child,' she protested, 'though I'm willing to admit I behaved childishly last night.' She did not look at him and fixed her eyes on the distant horizon. 'You were right when you accused me of ignoring you in the diningroom. I was angry with you because you – because you—' She hesitated and then said in a rush: 'I know I made a fool of myself falling into the swimming-pool, but there was no need to take pity on me.'

'Pity on you?'

'Yes. That's why you asked me to spend the day with you in Cannes, wasn't it?'

Hoping he would deny it, she was sad when he did nothing of the sort.

'I suppose Claire told you,' he said slowly. 'I should have

realized she would.'

There was a long pause and Jane was intensely aware of him beside her. She longed to get up and run away, but knew that to do so would make her appear even more childish. How could she be so irrational over him? How could *she*, who had always prided herself on her logic and sensible attitude to men, have allowed herself to become so emotionally involved with this stranger? For that was what he was, she told herself firmly, a stranger; a man she hardly knew, with whom she had spent no more than a few brief hours. He had been extremely nice to her, but viewing it objectively she saw he had done no more than any man would have done in similar circumstances – befriended a lonely little heiress who had made a fool of herself. He regarded her as a member of his own circle – albeit a young one – and as such had tried to help her.

She could not help wondering what his attitude would have been if the real Janey Belton had been here instead of herself, for Janey would have needed no befriending, no helping hand. Perpetually surrounded by luxury and cosseted by wealth, Janey had the belief that the world was her oyster, a belief that only someone in her position *could* have. With bitterness Jane acknowledged that it took more than the donning of clothes and the assuming of a name to bridge the gap between one social sphere and another.

'You can't blame me because of my reasons for asking you out yesterday.'

Stephen's voice broke into her reverie with such abruptness that she started visibly and her magazine fell to the floor. He bent to pick it up and placed it on her lap, remaining in the half-turned position so that he was looking at her.

'I came on this cruise because I was ordered to, not because I wanted to. My one intention was to be alone, and that seemed thwarted when I kept bumping into a silly little blonde. I had heard a great deal about her and I was quite sure I wouldn't like her, yet strangely enough I found her charming and exceedingly entertaining.' His thin mouth quirked in a smile and then straightened as if he realized that to laugh now might be misconstrued. 'Certainly I asked you out because I was sorry for you. Any man worthy of the name would be sorry for a girl who made a spectacle of herself. But you can't blame me because my invitation was prompted by sympathy. And anyway, if I hadn't felt sympathy I'd never have had the courage to ask you out.'

She was surprised at his use of such a word. 'Why would it require courage?'

'Because you're only nineteen. I'm almost old enough to be your father.'

With a superhuman effort she restrained herself from telling him her real age.

'You're only thirty-five,' she said. 'There's no reason to talk as if you're Methuselah.'

'Thanks,' he said gruffly. 'But age isn't always a question of years. Sometimes I feel so old and tired that I don't think I'll ever be able to enjoy anything again. When a man starts to think along those lines there are three courses open to him: work until he drops, drink until he's insensible or—' he hesitated '—or fall for a girl who's still young enough to feel the joy of life.' He pushed back his chair with a violent gesture and stood up, blotting out the sun. 'The problem is, Jane, that the first two courses don't appeal to me. Even if I wanted to work any more I can't. I've been warned to take it easy for the next few months, not to talk or think about business, and not even to look at a damned newspaper! As to drink . . .' he shrugged, 'I'm not the type. So that only leaves the third solution.'

She stared at him, not seeing any tenderness in his face, only a look of anger that he should find himself in this position. If ever a man did not want to be upset by his own emotions that man was Stephen Drake. Unwittingly she had, in some miraculous way, managed to infiltrate behind the wall he had built around himself, and he was hating her for it. Excitement welled in her, causing her body to tremble, her palms to grow damp. She did not know what to say and intuitively knew that to say nothing would be best.

'Come and sit down, Stephen.' Her voice was light and controlled, as if they had only been discussing the weather. 'You look tired, and it isn't good for you to stand in the sun.'

He sank down on his chair again and closed his eyes. A muscle at the side of his face was throbbing and beneath his tan the colour had drained from his face. There was no doubt that the doctors were right when they had ordered him to rest, for this scene between them had exhausted him. She longed to put out her hand and touch him, but knew that such a gesture would be unwelcome; for the moment she must allow any gesture to come from him. Fear and happiness warred within her, and the need to tell him the truth about herself was so strong that she could not bear it any longer.

'Stephen, I—'

'Excuse me, but would you be Miss Belton?' She turned sharply and saw a steward behind her, a blue and white envelope in his hand.

'Yes, I'm Janey Belton.'

'This cable has just come for you, miss.'

Handing her the envelope, he walked away, and Jane opened it quickly and read the message:

'MAN RECOVERED CONSCIOUSNESS FEW MINUTES ONLY BUT NO FURTHER INFORMATION STOP HAVE LEARNED PERSON IN QUESTION BOOKED AT LAST MOMENT STOP LOOK FOR NAMES NOT ON PASSENGER LIST STOP LOVING FATHER CEDRIC.'

Jane crumpled the telegram and, walking over to the rail, threw it overboard, watching the blue and white paper bob on the waves until it flattened out and disappeared.

'Look on the passenger list.' But there was no need for her

to do that, for she knew the person who had decided to come on the cruise at the last moment. Not only knew him but loved him. She swung round and looked at the recumbent figure a few yards away from her. 'Stephen,' she whispered. 'It can't be Stephen.'

Unsteadily she returned to her chair and sat down. It was impossible. What need would he have to steal the Lorenz Diamond, or to involve himself in any of the other robberies that had taken place? It could not be lack of money. Yet why else would he steal? Unbidden, the memory of one of their earlier conversations returned to her mind. 'The only thing that makes life worth living is the danger in it, the knowledge that it's *you* against everyone else, the knowledge that you can lose everything by one mistake.'

Could it be possible that Stephen, satiated with power, feeling there was no competitor his equal, had decided to pit his wits against Scotland Yard? It was so ridiculous an idea that she dismissed it from her mind. Love was making her fanciful. The only reason Stephen had boarded the ship at the last minute was because he had not wanted to come at all. There was no criminal reason behind it, no secret motivation other than a dislike of doing nothing for weeks on end; though from the look of him lying so pale and still beside her, if he had not followed his doctors' orders he would have collapsed. The strain of controlling an empire was too much for a man who knew himself to be alone, even if his loneliness was of his own making.

Beside her Stephen stirred. 'I must have fallen asleep. I'm sorry, Jane.'

'That's all right. You shouldn't get so het up about things. It's bad for you.'

'You sound like my doctors!' he laughed. 'I hope you're not going to start fussing over me?'

'Never. You're old enough to look after yourself.'

'You're not.' His gaze was contemplative. 'I'm surprised your father let you come away alone. A pretty girl shouldn't be allowed out without a chaperone.'

Nervously Jane wondered whether any news had leaked out of Janey's friendship with Ted Wills.

'I wouldn't let myself have a chaperone, thanks. Victoria's been dead a long time! Anyway, I'm used to being on my own.'

'Is your mother dead?' he asked gently.

'Yes.' Jane remembered her own mother and was overwhelmed with sadness. 'She died when I was fourteen. It's a bad age to lose a mother, particularly for a girl.'

'Any time's a bad age to lose a mother,' he said. 'I'm approaching senility, yet I'd hate to think of losing mine. You'll like my mother, Jane,' he said with a change of tone. 'She's an inveterate globetrotter, though, and I never know where she's going to be from one month to the next.'

'I'd like to meet her,' Jane said eagerly.

'I'll fix it up when we get back. I suppose you're staying on the ship all the time, are you?'

'Why, yes. I didn't know one could do anything else.'

'Some of the passengers are leaving at Athens. I intended to do the same, but I'm not sure now whether I will.'

Again there was a scowl on his face and again she said nothing. Getting Stephen to fall in love with her had been an accident, a happy stroke of fate, but getting him to admit it and accept it would require all her skill and feminine wiles.

She stood up. 'I'll go and change. It's nearly time for lunch.'

'What about meeeting me in the bar for a drink?'

'Do you think I'm old enough for more than orange juice?'

'From the subtle way you're handling me,' he said gruffly, 'I've a good mind to offer you Pernod!'

She was still smiling at his remark when she entered her cabin and changed into a green sundress. Her face was shiny, but she left it that way, only colouring her mouth with vivid coral lipstick that matched her nails. Short nails they were, broken by the typewriter, the fingers blunt and capable; not the hands of an heiress, she thought disconcertedly, and closed the cabin door behind her.

The bar was on the top deck next to the ballroom. One wall was made of glass and afforded a magnificent view of the horizon. Sitting on the scarlet and orange leather seats, one had the impression of riding the waves alone. As usual every seat was occupied and the noise overwhelming as she entered and looked round for Stephen. Disconcerted, she saw that he was sitting next to Colin and Claire, and she walked over to him.

Jane had been pleased with her appearance until now, but looking at the other girl she conceded the smartness of silk trews and shirt in matching scarlet, the waist banded by a wide black sash with long, fringed ends.

'She makes me feel as though I should be wearing broderie anglaise and baby talcum powder!' Jane thought crossly, and seeing the waiter hovering next to her defiantly ordered a Campari soda.

Stephen looked surprised. 'It's rather a bitter drink.'

'I prefer it to milk,' Jane said, annoyed as he saw him grin.

Colin coughed and proffered a packet of cigarettes. 'You'll be delighted to hear that we won our game of quoits. Claire's a dab hand at throwing the ring.'

'It's about time I tried to catch one,' Claire drawled. 'Seeing girls like Janey growing up makes me feel my age.'

'Come off it.' There was coldness in Colin's precise voice. 'A girl these days isn't old at twenty-seven.'

'A girl's as old as her experience.'

Listening to the conversation, Jane wondered whether there was more to it than appeared on the surface, for there was a raggedness in Claire's voice that spoke of ill-controlled temper. Could she really be worried that she was unmarried? She looked so beautiful with her glossy dark hair and pale madonna-like face that Jane dismissed the thought as ridiculous.

Claire leaned forward and picked up her drink, a mint *frappé*. Her hands curved round the glass and a heavy gold coin bracelet on one wrist clicked against the table.

'How lovely that is,' Jane exclaimed. 'I've always wanted a coin bracelet.'

'My father used to collect them,' Claire shrugged, 'and when he died my mother let me have these.'

Jane's scalp prickled with excitement. The noise of the people around her receded and her own thoughts seemed so loud that she was afraid lest they became audible.

'Can I have a look at the bracelet?' she asked casually.

Claire held out her hand and Jane examined the coins. Some were the size of shillings, some the size of half-crowns. Many of them were embossed and one or two inlaid with jewels, but there was none with an 'L', and Jane sat back in her seat. It had been a childish hope anyway. The criminal she was looking for would certainly not be a woman.

'I didn't know you were keen on coins,' Stephen said to her. 'I've a pretty good collection myself.'

'You have?' Jane's heart thumped. She wanted him to continue, yet was afraid of what he might say if he did.

'It's a hobby of mine,' he went on. 'At least it began as a hobby, but now it's almost an investment.'

'Things that start off as a hobby,' Colin interposed, 'often have the habit of either becoming an investment or an obsession. But I must say collecting coins has never particularly attracted *me*. Waterford glass, now, that's something I'm really keen on.'

Jane lost track of the conversation and wished with all her heart that she had never drawn attention to Claire's bracelet. Again suspicion grew within her and tugged at her mind with troubled fingers. Each doubt was caused by evidence as flimsy as chiffon, and yet chiffon could bind and hold and strangle.

'What about you, Janey?' Colin said.

She turned so quickly that her glass shook in her hand.

'I'm afraid I didn't hear the question.'

'We were talking about jewellery and Claire said you never wear any.'

'Maybe Janey's father thinks she's too young,' Claire drawled.

'Actually,' Jane drawled in exact imitation of Claire's voice, 'I have so much I'm bored with it. I've handed my jewel-case over to the Purser, and I've no intention of wearing any of it.'

Colin ran a hand over his silver-blond hair. 'What a pity. I think jewellery enhances a woman's beauty. Don't you, Stephen?'

'Some jewels do. But some are so beautiful in themselves that wearing them is only a detraction.'

'I know what you mean,' Claire replied. 'If I had all the money I wanted I think I'd collect jewels and just keep them in velvet-lined boxes.'

'Exactly,' Stephen said. 'Rubies and sapphires look their loveliest when seen against a background of black velvet. They lose their colour when worn against a woman's skin. The only jewel that improves by the wearing is the pearl.'

Jane listened to the conversation with fascinated horror. It seemed too much like a coincidence that in the last few hours there should be so many different fingers of suspicion pointing towards Stephen.

'What about diamonds?' she said in a voice that seemed too loud.

'Diamonds?' The dark eyes narrowed.

'Yes, diamonds. Are they the sort of jewel that looks best in a velvet-lined box?'

'That depends on the diamond,' came the smooth answer. 'Each one must be judged on its own merit. Large ones should never be worn, of course. At least if they're worn the best places for them are in a royal crown or sceptre. But the average woman would do well to stick to small stones of ten or twelve carats.'

'The average woman couldn't afford one or two carats!'

Jane replied dryly. 'But if most women were given the chance they'd wear the largest diamonds they could.'

'I agree with Stephen,' Claire said. 'Large diamonds don't look a bit pretty. I'd much rather have their equivalent in money tucked away in my bank.'

Both the men laughed at this, and Colin in particular seemed to find it amusing.

'It wouldn't be you who's stolen the Lorenz Diamond, would it?' he grinned.

Claire put down her drink. 'I value my life too much to do a stupid thing like that.'

'Why your life? There's no death sentence these days.'

'Maybe not, but you're put in prison, and that would be a death sentence to *me*. No, much as I'd like to possess jewellery I'm too lazy to go to the trouble of stealing it.'

'I can understand someone wanting to do it, though,' Stephen commented. 'All these treasures tucked away in museums must be a great challenge to people. I'm not just talking about jewels either, but *objets d'art* and paintings. I've often thought that if I'd been born into another time I'd have become a Raffles.'

Jane moistened lips that had suddenly become dry. 'Take from the rich to give to the poor? You could do that even now without becoming a thief.'

'Give my own money, you mean?' Stephen's head turned sharply. 'Ah yes, but it's dull just giving your money away like that. No, Jane, you can't talk me out of it. In my dreams I see myself as Robin Hood.'

Claire made some comment, but Jane was too shaken to join in the conversation. More than ever she was convinced of Stephen's guilt and she fought against it. She had nothing tangible to go on, only casual remarks which were capable of different meanings, depending on how one looked at them. 'And I'm looking at them with fear and suspicion,' she acknowledged. 'My very love for Stephen is making me biased against him.'

She was so immersed in her problems that it was not until

Stephen put his hand on her shoulder that she realized they were standing up, ready to go down to lunch.

'Unless you'd like another drink?' he said. 'You were late joining us and we're one up on you.'

'No more, thanks.' She stood up. 'I could do with some food.'

As they took their places in the dining-room Jane was glad to be sitting with Colin. At least she was saved the effort of having to pretend to an animation she did not feel. Indeed at the moment she was hard pressed not to rush back to her cabin and try and make some order out of her thoughts.

'What's the matter, Janey?' Colin asked. 'You seem upset about something. You haven't been quarrelling with Stephen, have you?'

'No. And there's nothing wrong, honestly there isn't.'

'Well, something's on your mind, then. Care to tell me about it?'

She shook her head, but saw from the obstinate look on his face that he was not to be satisfied. Early in their friendship she had realized he was no fool, and she had had no reason to change her opinion. Rather to the contrary, for the more she got to know him, the more she realized that he was a man of subtle perception. The last thing in the world she wanted was for him to start probing.

'As a matter of fact,' she said quickly, 'you were right. It *is* Stephen. We haven't quarrelled, but — well, I suppose you'll think I'm childish when I tell you that . . .' She stopped, desperately trying to make up some reason. But her hesitancy helped her, for in the pause Colin spoke again.

'You like the chap, don't you?' he said. 'It sticks out half a mile, so you needn't bother denying it.'

'Yes, I *do* like him. He's so different.'

'Different? I'd have thought you'd met many men of his type.'

'I've met lots of rich ones,' she said quickly, 'but none so young and attractive — present company excluded, of course.'

'Thanks for those kind words, Janey, but they're not necessary. When Stephen whisked you out of the ballroom last night, I knew he had the edge over me. Come on, tell Uncle Colin what you've quarrelled about and I'll see if I can help.'

'It wasn't a quarrel,' she said. 'It's just that there's so much I don't know about him.'

'That's no reason for you to look depressed,' Colin said in surprise. 'I thought you were going to tell me you'd had some ghastly row.'

'I knew you'd find it difficult to understand,' she sighed. 'You know all about the people in your own circle. I mean, you grew up with them and went to the same schools and attended the same dancing classes!'

'Don't tell me you didn't do the same?' He raised his eyebrows. 'You talk as if you'd come from a different world.'

'A different generation,' she said quickly. 'Stephen and I never went to the same dancing school.'

'I should think not. You were probably in your pram at the time! But is that what's worrying you – the fact that you didn't dance together as children?'

She laughed. 'Of course not. But I do wish I knew more about him.'

'So do a lot of other people,' Colin replied. 'Drake's always been a mystery man. He came from a moneyed background, but his father went through a fortune. He'd have gone through the lot if he could have got his hands on it, but a great deal of the money was in his wife's name. That's probably one of the reasons why he never walked out on her. Stephen was the only child, and from what I gather he hated his old man. As soon as he left Oxford he went abroad – Canada, I believe it was. He only came back when his father was ill. I remember hearing about it from a chap I knew. He said that Drake senior realized he couldn't keep control of his empire. There was talk of a take-over and I suppose he felt that unless there was someone to follow in his steps everything he'd built up would disappear. Anyway, Stephen came back and the two of them patched it up. But he never really got going on this tycoon stuff until his father died. It was as if the old man's death was a release for him, and from that moment he went from strength to strength.'

Jane sighed. 'I wonder if Stephen and his father had any real liking for each other at the end, or whether it was only a sense of duty and pride that brought them together.'

'Those are very often the only two emotions that exist between father and child,' Colin said cynically.

'Not amongst the men I know,' Jane retorted.

'Then we must mix in different circles.'

Realizing the truth of this, she said nothing, and Colin continued speaking.

'A lot of people have been curious as to what Stephen did when he was abroad, but no one's been able to find out. Some said he farmed near Vancouver, others that he was engaged in smuggling and gun-running in the Caribbean area!'

'I don't believe it.'

'Well, I can't see him farming,' Colin admitted. 'He's much more likely to do something that held danger.'

Jane's fork clattered to her plate. Strange that Colin should also feel that Stephen would be more likely to have an occupation involving danger. Did one feel this because of his virile looks or because one instinctively sensed the strongly leashed power, the tightly controlled aggressiveness?

'How long has he been in England?' she asked. 'I know he's been in the news over the last three years, but was he here before that?'

'About a year long, I think. As a matter of fact Claire mentioned it to me earlier today. She and Stephen were comparing notes about something and he said he'd been in England since August 1967.'

'August 1967?'

The words, innocuous though they seemed, pointed one more finger of suspicion in Stephen's direction. Or was it merely a fateful coincidence that the daring robberies of jewellery and *objets d'art* should have begun exactly four weeks after Stephen had set foot in his country again?

CHAPTER SEVEN

IMMEDIATELY lunch was over Jane's one desire was to plead a headache and return to her cabin, but in this she was thwarted, for, as she threw down her crumpled napkin and pushed back her chair, Stephen's voice spoke behind her.

'I've been trying to attract your attention the last five minutes,' he said.

She avoided looking directly at him. 'Did you want me for anything?'

'Do I have to have a special reason?' His voice was so low that only she could hear. 'I'd have liked you to have joined my table, but I can't alter the seating arrangements of my own accord. I'll speak to Dinky Howard about it this afternoon.'

'Don't do that,' she said quickly. 'It would be rude to Colin.'

'Blow Colin,' he said, and tempered his words by a smile in the direction of the man hovering on Jane's other side.

Sandwiched between the two of them, she walked out of the dining-room, relieved when Claire left her own table and joined them.

'What about a foursome at deck quoits?' she asked.

'I've got a headache,' Jane replied. 'I'm going to lie down in my cabin.'

'You should be in the fresh air,' Stephen said. 'Our chairs are reserved, so they'll still be vacant.'

Before she could protest, he edged her to the lift and within a few seconds they had ascended to the main deck.

Seated once more at her side, he looked at her so searchingly that she knew he would not be appeased until she had satisfied his curiosity.

'Have you really got a headache, or has Claire said something else to annoy you?'

'Claire hasn't said anything. No one has.'

'Then what's wrong? Why did you look at me with dislike when I came up to you in the dining-room just now?'

'I'm sorry, Stephen. It's nothing. Maybe I forgot to tell you I'm moody. Most girls of my age are.'

'Moodiness is not confined to girls of *your* age.' There was humour in his voice, but she did not respond to it and with a grunt he lay back and closed his eyes.

For a long while Jane pondered on all she had learned, but gradually tiredness overcame her and her eyelids drooped.

'My dear Miss Belton!' She was jerked into wakefulness by a lisping voice, and tilting her head saw Dinky Howard. Looking at him, his arms folded across his chest, his eyes twinkling, she was reminded of a bird: a magpie-cum-robin-redbreast with a touch of eagle!

'I've been wanting to talk to you, my dear Miss Belton, but you've been *so* busy with our *dear* Mr. Drake.' He glanced across at Stephen's recumbent form and lowered his voice to a whisper.

Jane glanced at Stephen and saw by the twitching of his lids that he was feigning sleep. Standing up she motioned the American to the far side of the deck.

'Of course,' Dinky Howard nodded as they moved across. 'We don't want to wake the dear man, *do* we? He's exhausted. *Exhausted.* I'm not surprised, though, when I consider the *pace* at which he works ... Not that I don't work hard *myself*, little lady. This sort of cruise takes a *great* deal of energy ...'

He meandered on, and Jane listened with a mixture of amusement and disbelief. Never would she have believed a character like Dinky existed outside a work of fiction. But here he was – large as life and twice as surprising.

'Of course, I promised your father I would keep an eye on you,' the unctuous voice continued, 'but when I saw that Mr. Drake was doing it *for* me I thought I'd leave you alone.' He laughed gently and tilted his head on one side, waiting for Jane to follow suit.

She did so, at the same time mentally composing another article for the *Morning Star*. What luck to be talking to Dinky Howard! Remembering the difficulty she had had in trying to persuade him to see her for a mere five minutes, she could not help being amused at the change in her position.

'You're not a bit like your father, of course,' Dinky Howard gushed on. 'I suppose you take after your mother?'

'Yes,' Jane answered automatically. 'How many people do you have on the cruise?'

Though taken aback by the change of conversation, he rallied well.

'Ninety-eight. Not many for a ship this size, I know, but then *everyone* has their own stateroom and I've a far *larger* crew than is usual. But this is a cruise *par excellence*. It's the third one I've organized and the demand grows greater and *greater*. Why, I had to turn down unbelievable numbers of people!'

'Really?' Jane said slowly. 'I thought Mr. Drake came on at the last minute.'

'Oh yes, but I always keep a few *extra* places tucked away for people of *importance*. Quite a few of my guests came on at the last moment.'

Her interest quickened. 'Anyone I know?'

'Why, yes. Colin Waterman. He booked some months ago, but cancelled it. However at the *last* moment he changed his mind again and I was able to fit him in. Quite confidentially, I think he was squiring some *girl* around town, but nothing came of it and he decided to come on this cruise *instead*.'

Jane was not surprised to hear this, for intuitively she had felt that Colin was looking for a chance to settle down. Indeed, until he had so easily accepted her feelings for Stephen, she had felt sure he had been considering her as a likely wife.

'The latest arrival, of course, hasn't yet joined the ship. He comes on at Monte Carlo tomorrow. Lord Rupert Copinger.'

Jane echoed the name, suddenly realizing why it sounded familiar: the young man Cedric Belton was hoping his daughter would marry!

'That's *one* reason I wanted to talk to you this afternoon, Miss Belton,' the American went on. 'I'd like to introduce Lord Rupert to you. Such a *charming* boy and such an *excellent* family.'

'Poor, though,' Jane said dryly.

'You mustn't be mercenary,' Dinky Howard twittered. 'Not every man has the ability to make a fortune the way your dear father has. Breeding and name mean a great deal, you know.'

'I'd rather have an exciting, dynamic proletarian,' Jane said dryly, 'than a well-bred bore!'

Dinky's beady eyes grew glassy. 'A sense of humour as well as beauty! No wonder your father has such *great* plans for you. I will enjoy introducing Lord Rupert to you.'

He minced away, but Jane remained where she was, aware of an overwhelming sense of relief. Stephen had not been the only passenger to board the ship at the last moment! There were Colin and Lord Rupert. Having strong reasons for guessing at Colin's sudden decision to come on the cruise, she dismissed him as a suspect, but Lord Rupert was still someone to be reckoned with. Unlikely though it was, he could be the man she was looking for; he was no more unlikely a suspect than Stephen. Indeed, he had one strong motivation that Stephen lacked: he was notoriously hard up.

Light-heartedly she returned to her chair where Stephen, realizing the coast was clear, was now sitting up.

'You might at least have come to my rescue,' she protested.

'Nothing would have helped you! Dinky was watching

you like a lynx all morning and I knew he was anxious to get you alone. What did he want?'

'To tell me Lord Rupert Copinger's coming on board.'

'Good lord! That idiot?'

'Do you know him?'

'Reasonably well. Not that there's much to know. Five minutes' conversation with him and the rest is repetition! Don't tell me Dinky's got him lined up for *you*.'

'Not Dinky,' she replied. 'My father. He'd like me to marry a title.'

'And what about you? Don't you fancy yourself as Lady Something or other?'

'If I loved the man – yes. But not otherwise.'

He looked at her searchingly and she returned his gaze without any change of expression.

'You've recovered, haven't you?' he said suddenly. 'You're not moody any more.'

'I told you I'd be better if you left me alone.'

'I know you did. And I'm glad you're right. I only hope you won't put me in your black books again too soon.'

Although she remained smiling, Jane silently echoed his words, hoping desperately that the suspicions she had felt about him could be directed towards someone else.

The *Cambrian* docked at Monte Carlo at eight a.m. the next morning, but Jane, anxious to appear blasée, did not go on deck until nearly ten. A few of her co-passengers had already disembarked, though Claire and Colin, together with a newly-wed Texan couple, were sipping coffee by the pool.

As usual Claire looked soignée in Pucci pants of tangerine silk with a white shirt, and she gave Jane a mocking glance as she approached.

'I can see *you're* going ashore,' she said. 'You've got that expectant look about you!'

Jane flushed. 'As a matter fact I am. I've never been to Monte Carlo.'

'Really? I thought your school spent a summer here? Belinda mentioned something about a *château* in the hills.'

The flush on Jane's cheeks deepened. 'It must have been the term I was – the term I was away with measles.'

'How awful to get measles when you're a teenager,' Colin intervened. 'I had it when I was fifteen and felt an awful ass.'

Jane looked at him gratefully, certain that he knew Claire was trying to bait her. Or did he suspect she was only pretending to be who she was? She dismissed the thought instantly and, deciding his defence of her was due to kindness and nothing else, gave him an extra warm smile.

'We're going ashore too,' he said. 'Spending the day at the Sporting Club. Care to come along?'

Jane nodded, hoping against hope that Stephen would accompany them. Almost as the thought entered her mind she saw him walking along the deck towards them.

'I thought you'd gone ashore without me.' He spoke to them all, but looked at Jane.

'We'd never go without you, darling,' Claire drawled, and stood up, stretching herself like a cat.

The tight line of her pants emphasized every curve, and the eyes of the men were upon her, Stephen's glance as admiring as the rest. Jane knew a stab of jealousy and she walked to the gangplank and descended to the harbour.

If she had been delighted with Cannes, she was enthralled by her first view of Monte Carlo. Beyond the tree-lined promenade honey-coloured houses mounted tier upon tier up the hill, while flanking one side stood the great Rock, atop of which perched the fairy-tale palace of Monaco with its gaily-coloured sentry boxes and stone turrets.

'How about a drive before we get settled?' Colin suggested. 'If Janey hasn't seen Monte Carlo before I'm sure she'd like to have a look at it.'

Jane nodded and he signalled a couple of *fiacres*. She was disappointed to see Stephen commandeered by the Texan and his wife, although her disappointment was mitigated by the fact that Claire was forced to join herself and Colin.

They set off at an easy pace and spent the next few hours exploring the small stretch of coast. Jane began to understand why it was called the Land of Palm Trees and Mimosa, for the scent of flowers was overpowering, while no matter what narrow road they turned into or what steep hills they climbed, there was always the brilliance of blossoms and the shade of palms. But the intense colour of the scene, the glaring whiteness and the brilliant greens and reds made her eyes ache, and she was glad when they paused for a drink in the little hilltop of Roquebrune.

Iced drinks finished, they drove back along the coast and around Monte Carlo itself. Jane was surprised to find that it covered only a few hundred square yards and seemed largely made up of hotels and restaurants, its centre broken by a pretty square fronting the world-famous Casino. Fabulous Monte Carlo – home of the rich, hopeful Mecca of the poor!

It was just noon when they reached the Sporting Club and settled themselves around the turquoise swimming-pool, set with white chairs and gaudy parasols. An orchestra played to one side and waiters flitted between the sunburnt men and women.

Lunch was a gay affair, interspersed with light wine and lighter conversation, after which they retired to the beach huts and changed into swimming costumes.

Jane wore the inevitable bikini, a white broderie anglaise one this time, piped with scarlet. A red bandana held back her blonde hair and scarlet-tipped toenails gleamed from beneath gold sandals.

Although too pale-skinned to acquire the same deep tan as Claire, she was nonetheless delighted with her honey-gold appearance and was happily conscious of the admiring male glances that followed her as she rejoined her party. Stephen was the only one who had already changed, and though she had seen him in swimming trunks before, her new-found love for him made her intensely aware of his appearance. Never had she seen anyone whose physique was more symbolic of his character, for the words that one could have used to describe his personality would have applied equally well to his looks. The broad shoulders and chest, the narrow hips and strong, sinewy legs exuded the same dynamic forcefulness, while the firm column of his neck and the carriage of his head, with its rough black hair, bespoke a proud sensitivity.

If she were guilty of staring at him, he was equally guilty of staring at her, and embarrassed colour flooded into her face.

'I didn't know girls still blushed,' he murmured. 'You're a strange mixture, Jane.'

'Don't you like it?'

'I more than like it, as you very well know.' He waited until she was lying on the mattress beside him. 'It's a funny thing, but since meeting you I've realized something I've always refused to acknowledge until now.'

'What's that?'

'That newspapers can lie!'

She burst out laughing. 'According to my father they're lying all the time!'

'As a newspaper proprietor I can't be expected to agree with *that*.' He grinned. 'Seriously, though, you're so different from what I'd expected.'

Again he was repeating himself and again she felt a tremor of anxiety as she wondered what he would say when he discovered the truth. Would his feelings for her overcome his pride or were they too new to withstand the shock of discovering that she was not an heiress? Not that the lack of money would be a deterrent; if Stephen loved a woman he would disregard her background. What he could not disregard would be deceit.

'Now you're looking moody again,' he teased. 'Come on, Jane. You didn't have much lunch. Let's go for a swim.'

Claire, approaching silently, picked up the last sentence. 'Don't tell me you're going to get Janey into the water at last!' she drawled.

With a start Jane recalled that she was supposed to be afraid of the water. What a good thing Claire had mentioned it. Otherwise she would more than likely have given a beautiful display of aquatics!

'Of course Jane's going in,' he replied. 'She's not scared with me.'

Pulling her to her feet, he led her over to the pool.

'I'll have a quick dip first,' he said, 'and give you a chance to come in. If you're like most non-swimmers I expect you'll do it a toe at a time.'

He dived in and swam to the far side, leaving Jane to sit on the edge. She longed to dive in too, but realizing it would give the game away, did what Stephen expected and inched herself into the pool. It was a painful process, for her body had been warmed by the sun and the water struck cold, but gritting her teeth, she gradually immersed and then ducked in completely.

'Good girl,' Stephen called, and swam back towards her.

There began for Jane one of the most difficult half-hours she had ever spent, as she pretended to a fear she did not have and a clumsiness she did not feel. But gradually she dropped both reactions, and taking the chance that Stephen might guess she had fooled him, she started to do the breast-stroke properly. However, she need not have worried over his reactions, for with typical masculine ego, he assumed her amazing progress to be the result of his own tuition.

'I've never known a girl catch on so quickly,' he said. 'Have a shot at swimming the width.'

'I don't think I could,' she protested.

'Of course you can. Come along.'

Realizing this was one more nail of deceit in her coffin of lies, she did so, rewarded to hear Stephen clap as she reached the far side.

'I'll have you a first-class swimmer in no time,' he called. 'Now you've done enough for the moment. Go and lie in the sun.'

Obediently Jane returned to the mattress, leaving him to continue his swim. The rest of the party were also in the water and she watched enviously as they dived and somersaulted. Claire was certainly a wonderful swimmer and took every opportunity of showing off, making sure she remained as close to Stephen as she could.

It seemed an eternity, yet it could only have been ten minutes, before Stephen came out of the pool and walked towards her. He was half-way when he was hailed by a pudgy-faced young man on a Lilo, and after a brief conversation they both came across to her.

'I'd like you to meet a new passenger,' Stephen explained. 'He's been here a couple of days waiting for us to arrive. Lord Rupert Copinger – Miss Janey Belton.'

Jane restrained a desire to giggle, for it would have been difficult to find anyone who more resembled their name than Lord Rupert. Tall and gangling, with large, knobbly joints and frizzy hair on his chest and head, he gave the appearance of a badly manipulated puppet.

Was this the man Cedric Belton had lined up for his high-spirited daughter? Ted Wills, no matter what he looked like, could not be worse!

'Delighted to meet you,' Lord Rupert said in a high-pitched voice. 'I've heard a lot about you.' He squatted down on the mattress beside her and smiled, showing large teeth that added to his unprepossessing appearance.

'I shouldn't believe all you've heard,' Jane said shortly, and tried to rid herself of the antipathy she felt towards him.

'Oh, but I do,' he said. 'I'm a very trusting person.'

'How long have you been here?' Stephen intervened, deliberately changing the subject.

'I told you – two days – and before that I was in Biarritz. I was going to join the *Cambrian* in London, but I had to leave England earlier.'

'An irate father after you?' Stephen quipped.

Lord Rupert shook his head. 'An irate bookmaker.

Money's the very devil. Every time I lay my hands on some I swear I'm going to save it – but I never can.' He ran a bony hand through his hair. 'Sometimes I think I'll have to get another job.'

'*Another* one?' Stephen raised his eyebrows. 'I never knew you were in one.'

'Oh yes. I worked for a publicity firm. Wet nursing elderly Americans. I stuck it for quite a while, but eventually I forgot to be polite, and they fired me. But I'm not sorry. I needed a holiday after all that work, so I booked on the *Cambrian*.'

Jane wondered where a self-confessed pauper had obtained the money for such a cruise; yet many society people in the same financial straits seemed able to do what they wanted regardless of cost. Claire was a prime example, though there were admittedly many ways for a woman to acquire money ... Her glance slid over Lord Rupert and moved quickly away again. Not even for his title could she imagine any self-respecting woman warming to him.

'I must say I was surprised to find *you* on board,' Lord Rupert remarked to Stephen.

'Doctors' orders. And damned tedious ones too. At least they would have been if I hadn't met Jane.'

Vacant grey eyes stared at her. 'Ah yes, Jane. My favourite name for a girl. Old-fashioned but charming.' Once more his large teeth showed in a smile. 'Would you like to come in for a swim?'

'I've just been in, thanks.' Not caring that he might consider her rude, she lay back and closed her eyes. The two men spoke desultorily for a while and then she felt a shadow on her face as they got up and moved away. Within a moment Stephen came back and sat down again.

'Well, that's got rid of him,' he said softly. 'What an ass he is.'

Jane opened her eyes. 'Where's he gone?'

'I edged him over to the pool and introduced him to Claire. Luckily she'd never met him before.' He turned his head. 'Damn. It didn't take *her* long to decide he's no use!'

Jane followed his gaze and saw Lord Rupert sitting dejectedly at the side of the pool, his knobbly knees half immersed in the water.

'Fancy Cedric—' she stopped. 'Fancy my father thinking I could fall for him. I couldn't even fancy him pickled!'

'Pickled he mightn't seem so bad,' Stephen replied. 'But stone cold sober he's impossible! Mind you,' he went on, 'I've often thought it unbelievable that anyone could be quite as stupid as Rupert.'

'What do you mean?'

'Merely that he's occasionally done a few things that haven't fitted in with the picture. We belong to the same club and we've sometimes played poker together. For an idiot, he's a surprisingly good player.'

Jane pondered the words as she continued to rub oil on herself. 'Why would someone pretend to be a fool? It doesn't make sense.'

'Why not? It's a great advantage to be underestimated. I've often wished people didn't give *me* credit for more brains than I've got. You can be far more clever if your ability isn't known.'

'I hadn't thought of that,' she said slowly. 'But I see what you mean.'

Indeed she did see what he meant, saw things he had not meant either, things that only she herself could see.

'When you said Lord Rupert often came into large sums of money, how much did you mean?' she asked.

'Mercenary, aren't you?' There was a slight coldness in his voice. 'Even you would consider them large. Last year, for example, he hired a lodge in Scotland for the grouse season, and at the rate he entertained he got no change from twenty thousand pounds.'

The grouse season. August the twelfth. Was it coincidence that in the July of last year a priceless jewelled cross had been stolen from the private collection of a millionaire in Suffolk? She remembered her father talking about it and explaining that thefts of that sort were the most difficult to recover.

'At least one can trace a painting or a vase, but when one is dealing with a diamond cross, it's well nigh impossible. The whole thing can be broken down and the stones sold singly or even re-cut.'

Was it possible that Lord Rupert could be the man she was looking for? It was no more impossible than that Stephen could be the suspect. She replaced the lid on the bottle of oil and lay down, marshalling the facts as she knew them. According to Janey Belton, Lord Rupert had been lined up as a prospective suitor. That meant he was anxious to marry money. He was perennially hard up, yet came into large sums which, instead of saving, he lavishly spent. How could one acquire large sums of money spasmodically? Gambling was one answer. Yet was Lord Rupert a known gambler? She turned her head and looked at Stephen, who was leaning back on the mattress beside her, smoking a cigarette.

'Does Lord Rupert gamble much?'

'Not as far as I know. He's not one of these perennial gamblers, if that's what you mean.'

At least that answered one question in her mind. But if he was not a gambler then where did he procure those sums of money? Her suspicion of him grew, and as it grew, so did her excitement. Yet was Lord Rupert sufficiently intelligent to be a good enough thief not to be caught? From his conversation he appeared a complete fool, and yet, if he were a complete fool, how did he get such large amounts of money?

Jane sat up and hugged her knees. Was it possible that Lord Rupert Copinger was only pretending to be simple-minded? Indeed, she found it difficult to believe that anyone could be quite such an ass as he was. What if the whole thing were an act? If he were using his idiocy merely as a cloak to hide an extremely subtle and ingenious mind? After all, who would suspect an aristocrat of being a thief, particularly if that aristocrat were well known for his stupidity? The more she thought about it, the more convinced Jane became that Lord Rupert was as good a suspect as Stephen. A better suspect, in fact, because she did not love him and would be delighted if she could shift her suspicions from one man to the other.

In front of her, Lord Rupert swung his legs away from the side of the pool and stood up. He remained for a moment where he was, looking around him uncertainly, and then, suddenly becoming aware of Jane watching him, he grinned vacantly and waved.

Feeling herself to be all kinds of a hypocrite, Jane gave him a wide, come-hither smile to which he responded by striding over to her.

'You should have come in for a swim,' he said with the eagerness of a puppy. 'The water was awfully warm.'

'I'm sure it was, but I was too tired. You could be an angel and offer to buy me a drink, though. I'm terribly thirsty.'

'I'd be delighted to. Shall we stroll over and have it at the bar?'

'Lovely.'

Conscious of Stephen turning his head sharply to look at her, Jane stood up and allowed Lord Rupert to take her arm.

'I won't be long, Stephen,' she said.

'Be as long as you like,' he replied coolly, and turned over on his stomach as she walked away.

CHAPTER EIGHT

JANE spent a boring and unrewarding hour with Lord Rupert. He added nothing further to what she already knew about him, beyond confirming her suspicions that no one could be so foolish unless it was by intent.

'Won't you find it dull not doing anything at all?' she asked as they sipped their orange juice at a small table overlooking the beach.

'I've still got the estate to attend to,' he replied. 'Mama does most of it, though, because I hate anything to do with farming. But when my publicity job ended I decided I'd had enough work for a while. That's why I came on this cruise. I must say you're even prettier than I'd expected.'

'I didn't know you'd expected me to be anything.'

'Oh yes. Your father told me . . .' He stopped and turned red.

'I didn't know you'd met my father,' Jane said, looking at him with innocent eyes.

'It was a few months ago at my club – he said you were going on this cruise.'

For a moment Jane wondered whether Cedric Belton could be paying for Lord Rupert's trip. If he were intent on his daughter marrying a title it would be one way of achieving it.

'I'm surprised Daddy never mentioned your name to me,' she went on. 'He's awfully keen on titles.'

Lord Rupert seemed surprised that she should mention such a thing.

'It's because he came up the hard way,' Jane continued. 'Men of Daddy's type think a title's more important than anything else in the world. But personally I consider the whole thing a nuisance. I mean, what do you do with it these days?'

'It's invaluable if you want to go into business with Americans.'

'Well, I don't want to go into business with Americans.'

Lord Rupert laughed uproariously and she glanced surreptitiously across to Stephen, seeing with irritation that Claire had joined him.

'Do have another drink,' Lord Rupert said, interrupting her thoughts.

'I don't want any more orange juice, thanks.'

'Then let me order something exotic for you.' He signalled for the waiter. 'I know just the sort of drink for you. Champagne and peach juice.'

'That sounds frightfully exotic and expensive.'

Lord Rupert tilted his head in an arrogant gesture that made him look like a well-bred horse. 'What's money for if not to be spent on a pretty girl?'

She nodded, too bored to continue the conversation, and watched as he conferred with the waiter, telling him the exact proportions of champagne to peach juice which he required. They sat silently in the hot, glaring sun until their drinks arrived, and she sipped hers, her nose wrinkling with appreciation.

'Hm, it really *is* good.'

'It's a little thing I picked up from an American I know.'

He continued to chatter vacuously and again she wondered whether it was an act. But to continue talking with him would not give her the answer, and she decided to cable her father and ask him to let her know all he could about Rupert Copinger. If his answer substantiated her own suspicions she would watch him carefully. If it did not, she would have to look elsewhere.

Her eyes returned to Stephen, jealously rising strongly as she saw Claire leaning close to him, one arm on his shoulder.

She pushed back her chair and Lord Rupert stood up. 'You're not going to leave me, are you, Janey? I thought we'd have lunch together.'

'The sun's given me a headache. I want to go back under the shade.'

'I'll get you an umbrella. Don't go.'

He rushed off, all arms and legs, and Jane waited until he was out of sight before walking back to her mattress.

Stephen did not look at her as she sat down and Claire continued her low-toned conversation with him.

'I'll change into a dry suit,' she said in a louder voice, 'and I'll be right back.'

With a supple gesture she got to her feet, but even when she had gone Stephen did not turn to look at Jane.

'Lord Rupert's an awfully silly young man,' she said casually. 'He talks on and on and says absolutely nothing.'

'I thought you realized that when you first met him. I'm surprised you needed further confirmation.'

Deciding it was ridiculous to pretend she did not know he was annoyed, Jane brought the reason into the open.

'There's no need to be cross just because I had a drink with him.'

'My dear, you're free to have a drink with anyone you like. I merely found it strange that one minute you say Rupert's a bore and the next minute you rush off for a *tête-à-tête* with him.'

'He asked me for a drink and I couldn't refuse.'

'You were ogling him while he was at the pool. I saw it.'

It was useless to deny the truth. She bit her lip, wishing she could tell him the reasons for her behaviour.

'Anyway, Jane, there's no reason for you to justify yourself with me. If you'd prefer to be with Rupert by all means go. It'll at least satisfy your father.'

'You can't blame me for my father's actions,' she protested.

'I can blame you for carrying them out! Not that I do blame you,' he said hastily. 'As I've just told you, you're free to do as you wish.'

Her reply was forestalled by Claire's return, and Stephen stood up and walked towards her.

'I never believed you when you said you wouldn't be long,' he said.

'I'm hungry, that's why. Come on now, where's that lunch you promised me?'

With her hand on his arm they walked away, and Jane, her cheeks burning, remained behind. How rude of them to ignore her, for she was, after all, a member of their party. She glanced round and saw the Texan couple having a drink at the bar with Colin.

'I might as well join them,' she thought, and was threading her way through the tables when she was hailed by Lady Pendlebury. Even in the Riviera sunshine, miles away from England, there was no mistaking the woman's background, for nothing could have been more symbolic of her class than her linen skirt and blouse, the white gloves on the table next to her white handbag and the battered white felt hat with its brim pulled uncompromisingly down over her greying hair. Her husband sat perspiring beside her, and he waved genially as his wife heralded Jane.

'Come and join us for a drink, child,' Lady Pendlebury called. 'We never see anything of you except in the dining-room.'

Knowing herself caught and not wishing to be rude, Jane sat down at the table with them. Maybe she would find some copy for the *Morning Star*. Sir Brian was always good for a controversial quote of the Colonel Blimp variety.

'I saw you talking to dear Rupert just now,' Lady Pendlebury went on. 'Such a charming boy. I was at school with his mother. Maybe you could go and find him, Brian, and see if he'd like to join us for lunch?'

Sir Brian disappeared in the direction of his wife's pointing hand and the two women were left alone.

'A most eligible young man,' Lady Pendlebury droned on. 'Poor, of course, but then so many of the better families are these days. But a dear boy who tries desperately hard to help his mother and sisters. Not cut out for business, though.' She looked at her husband's broad, retreating back in a disapproving way that said more than words. 'I know his mother hopes he'll settle down with some nice girl who'll be able to help him.'

'Help him?' Jane asked gently. 'In what way?'

Lady Pendlebury hesitated, not sure how guileless the question was.

'In all the ways a wife *can* help her husband,' she replied. 'After all, though Rupert hasn't any money he has other things to offer. Breeding and background and a title are important these days.'

'Yes. Lord Rupert told me so.'

'And he should know.' Lady Pendlebury laughed. 'For the last few years he's used it to great benefit. He organized safaris to Kenya. Can you imagine poor Rupert doing that when he absolutely loathes anything to do with animals? His mother thought it terribly brave of him and I must say I agree. For the last three years the poor boy's been rushing all over Kenya with rich Americans.'

'I thought he was in publicity,' Jane said.

'He was. At least it was the firm who did all the advertising. They put little notices in American papers: "Lord Rupert Copinger has room for a few additional guests on his next safari to Kenya." You know the sort of thing I mean.'

Jane nodded, her thoughts chaotic. If Rupert had been in Kenya for the last three years surely he would not have had the opportunity to commit the burglaries? Or had his trips to Kenya been for the main purpose of disposing of the articles he had stolen? Lady Pendlebury's next words, however, answered the unspoken question.

'His mother missed him dreadfully. She's terribly attached to Rupert, and not to see him even for a day for three years was really most trying for her. Still, he's back in England now and we all hope he'll settle down and find something really worth while to do.'

Jane sighed. Much though she would have liked Lord Rupert to be a suspect, Lady Pendlebury had completely exonerated him from guilt. She would have to think again.

The thought of suffering Rupert at lunch, when there was no longer any need, was more than she could bear and, blurting out an incoherent apology, she retreated in the direction of Colin who, with the Texan couple, was moving away from his bar stool.

'I was just coming over to rescue you,' he said as she came within earshot.

'If I'd known I'd have remained where I was,' she replied. 'I'm sure Lady Pendlebury thinks I'm mad.'

'Better be mad than bored.' He glanced behind her. 'And you would have been bored, I can tell you. Lord Rupert's just arrived.'

'I know. That's why I ran away!'

Colin laughed and caught her arm. 'Well you're in time for lunch. And then how about going in a speedboat afterwards?'

'Sounds lovely.'

Jane had never been in a speedboat before and she was enthralled with the experience, loving the fierce tug of the wind at her hair, the sharp feel of the spray on her skin and the exhilaration of speed that made her body tingle. She could have stayed out on the water for hours, but eventually the Texan girl declared that she wanted to rest, and they returned to the shore.

Without the wind taking away the heat it seemed hotter than ever, and Jane was glad to lie under the shade of a parasol and close her eyes. Clare and Stephen were not to be seen, and their absence increased her depression. Better at least for them to be here, where she could know what they were doing, than for them to be out of sight. She did not blame Stephen for being annoyed with her. In his position she would have felt the same. If only she had not told him Cedric Belton had lined Rupert up as a would-be suitor, and she had not made disparaging remarks about him, for all this had made her subsequent behaviour even more inexplicable. No wonder Stephen had put the wrong interpretation on it.

How complicated life was. And yet it could have been so happy. What more could one have asked from fate than to go on a cruise with unlimited clothes and the company of a man like Stephen? If only she had not had to worry about the Lorenz Diamond. Yet had it not been for the diamond she would not have been on the cruise at all, and Janey Belton would have been forced to go. Somehow she knew Stephen would have had nothing in common with the real Belton heiress, for she was like many of the women in his circle – rich, spoilt and uncaring for anyone except themselves.

She turned over on her stomach and rested her head in her arms. Was the Lorenz Diamond on board, or had the thief already smuggled it out of England? And if so, was he on his way to pick it up? What would he do with it once it was in his possession? Maybe even now it was reposing in a velvet-lined box in some hidden recess of Stephen's house.

Without realizing it, she groaned, and Colin lifted his head up.

'You all right, Janey?'

She turned. 'I must have been dreaming.'

'It's that lobster you had! What you need is a nice cup of tea.'

'What I need is exercise. I've never done so much lazing around in my life.'

'You talk as if this was your first holiday in years,' he laughed.

'Even though I don't work I'm always busy at home,' she told him.

'I'm sure you are.' His voice was teasing. 'But even so, you're one of the world's spoilt darlings who've never had to worry about money.'

'And you have, I suppose?'

114

Colin's eyes narrowed, making him look older and serious. 'Yes, I have – in the last few years, anyway.'

'When we first met you told me you weren't worried about the future.'

'I'm not really worried. It's just that ... Oh, let's forget it.'

'Is there anything I can do to help?'

As she spoke Jane wished she were actually Janey Belton and in a position to do something for him; as a reporter living on her salary she had no hope of helping him. Yet she had felt impelled to say something and she was rewarded when she saw the pleasure on his face.

'What a sweet thing to say, Janey. But don't get me wrong. I'm not short of money. It's just that sometimes one sets oneself a goal and is then so busy achieving it that one doesn't see that the goal is moving further away with every step one takes towards it.'

Jane knew he was speaking in allegorical terms, knew too that if she questioned him further she would learn nothing. Yet feminine perversity impelled her to do so.

'What *was* your goal, Colin?'

'I had two,' he replied. 'The first was a woman and the second was enough money to keep her happy.'

'I should have thought the second goal was easy,' she said, and remembered how happy her own parents had been, living within an income that Colin would have considered ludicrously inadequate. For the first time since she had come on the cruise she was irritated into indiscretion. 'So much talk about money! So much pretence and indolence. Gosh, you all work so hard trying not to be bored and trying to pretend you're all as rich as kings that ...' She stopped, aware of his amazement. 'I'm sorry, Colin, I—'

'Don't apologize for being your father's daughter,' he said drily. 'I don't wonder you find us a poor lot. We are, you know. And though I grant you that riches are relative, you can't keep the Queen of Sheba unless you're King Solomon. And now,' he said, standing up in one swift movement, 'I'll go and get you that cup of tea.'

He walked away, his pale hair more grey than blond in the sunlight. Their conversation had been surprising, showing her an aspect of his character she had not suspected until now. By most standards Colin was not a poor man and by her own standards he was a rich one. Yet he was dissatisfied because he did not have enough to possess the woman he loved. She sat up and rested her head against her bended knees. 'The Queen of Sheba,' he had said in describing the woman he loved. Curiously, she wondered who his Queen of Sheba could be.

It was not until dusk that Jane and Colin returned to the *Cambrian*. In the purple gloom the ship looked like a fairy-tale palace, lights ablaze as it floated on the sapphire blue water. Music wafted out on the still air and from the bar came the chink of ice in glasses and the buzz of voices.

Dinky Howard was poised at the top of the gangway and he chirped excitedly as they came into view.

'I'm so glad you got back early. There'll be great excitement tonight and I don't want you to be tired. We're having a fancy dress party.'

'What a pity you didn't tell us before,' Jane said. 'I haven't a thing to wear!'

'That's what all the women say,' Dinky Howard laughed. 'But if I'd told you earlier you'd have rushed to the shops and bought something elaborate, whereas this way you'll have to rely on your inventiveness, and that's *much* more fun. Dinner's at the usual time and the party itself begins at ten.'

He minced away, and Jane looked at Colin with dismay.

'I haven't really a thing to wear. Not one of my dresses can be altered.'

'I'm sure you'll find something.' He looked at her speculatively and then snapped his fingers. 'I've got it! We can go as a pair. I'll dress up as a pirate and you can be my captive – the Princess Fatima. Have you a gauzy sort of dress?'

'Will chiffon do?'

'Perfectly. But darken your skin a bit and smother yourself in jewellery.'

'I haven't got any.'

Colin stared at her. 'I thought you'd given your jewel-case to the Purser?'

'I have, and I don't want to wear any. I may lose it.'

'It's insured, isn't it?'

'Yes – but I don't like wearing jewellery.'

Irritation flickered in the grey eyes. 'You don't have to like it in order to wear it! And if you won't put any on it'll spoil the whole effect. I'm supposed to have *captured* you for your jewellery!'

Realizing that it would seem strange if she continued to demur, Jane presented herself at the Purser's office for her jewel-case, and Colin walked back with her to the cabin.

'It wasn't such a terrible thing to get it out, was it?' he said, tapping the lid. 'You must make yourself look as expensive as possible, so mix it all up if you can. Pearls and diamonds and rubies and—'

'Hey, I'm not the Woolworth heiress!'

'Maybe not. But you look as if you've got a pretty good collection in there. Open it and let me see. If I leave it to you I'm sure you'll arrive wearing one rope of pearls.'

Carefully Jane inserted the key in the jewel-case and lifted the lid. A necklace of rubies, each one the size of a farthing, gleamed redly up at her, while underneath it a rope of diamonds glittered like a neon snake.

'I can see why you don't like wearing these,' Colin murmured. 'They're a bit much for a girl of your age.'

'That's what I told my father, but he wouldn't listen. You can't blame him. He's got no other woman to dress up.'

Colin lifted out the ruby necklace and then the diamond one, his hands as gentle as if he were handling a baby.

'Wear both of these, but with the diamond earrings, and try and fasten some jewels in your hair. Oh, and put on all the bracelets too.'

'Would you like me to fasten a few around my ankle?' she joked.

'Most certainly. In for a penny, in for a pound!'

'In for half a million you mean.' The smile left her face as she entered her cabin and closed the door. Carefully she put the jewel-case on the dressing-table and looked at it. How stupidly careless of Janey not to have taken it with her.

The knowledge that a master criminal was on board, possibly not more than a stone's throw away, increased her apprehension. Here, within his grasp, lay yet another fortune, and all of it in jewels that could easily be broken down and sold.

'It's back to the Purser with that as soon as the party's over,' she vowed. She certainly had no intention of going to bed that night with the jewellery in her cabin.

Jane decided not to go down to dinner, for it would mean changing twice, and instead she ordered it in her cabin, using the time before it arrived to write a further article for her paper.

This time she concentrated on Dinky Howard and, feeling no compunction whatever, penned what she considered to be her best satirical piece. She wondered what Frank Preston would think of it, for she had known him tear to shreds some of her best copy and yet accept without a murmur stuff which she considered her worst. But that was like all features editors the world over, she thought, as she wrote the final line and quickly stuffed the article into a drawer as the steward came in with a tray.

As soon as she had finished eating, she pulled out three chiffon dresses from the wardrobe and laid them on the bed, staring at them critically as she decided which one to wear.

Her choice fell on the most exotic, a harem-skirted chiffon in pink and lavender, with a silver lamé underskirt adding a delicate lustre. Carefully she stepped into it and did up the minute hooks and eyes. It was no easy task, and she was panting and flushed by the time she had finished. Only as she came to the last hook did she chide herself for not having rung for the maid.

'You're not used to gracious living,' she addressed her reflection. 'That's your trouble, Jane Berry.'

But her reflection gave no hint of this and looked back at her, aloof and exotic.

Remembering Colin's instructions to make up more heavily than usual, she enjoyed herself slapping blue eyeshadow on her lids and outlining her eyes with black liquid. Then came the jewellery – the diamond necklace and the ruby one burned with their own fires around her neck while long pendant earrings flashed and glittered each time she turned her head. Ruby and diamond bracelets sparkled on one ankle and her left arm was heavy with emeralds and sapphires. It was not easy to place jewels in her hair, for she was terribly afraid of losing some of them during the dancing, and instead she piled her hair on the top of her head and entwined a long rope of pearls around it.

When she was ready she felt inexplicably shy, reluctant to face the curious eyes that would be upon her from the moment she left the cabin; but knowing Colin would come looking for her if she did not put in an appearance, she left her stateroom and went slowly up to the ballroom.

She stopped on the threshold, enjoying the colourful scene and amazed at the ingenuity of the costumes. Nurses danced with toy soldiers and a clown was clasping an ondine, who in turn was making eyes at a fearsome-looking teddy bear in a gold mohair coat! It was impossible to recognize anyone, and though she kept a lookout for a pirate it was not until Colin himself hailed her that she was able to recognize him.

He had spared no effort to look the part, but his costume showed no sign of improvisation and she guessed that the cocked hat and frilled silk shirt he wore had been brought along specifically for such a purpose. Indeed, now that she looked around she could see that many of the costumes were far too elaborate to have been invented at such short notice. Fancy dress was a part of every ship's cruise, and she was surprised that Janey had not prepared for it. Not that she need have worried at her own appearance, for Colin's gaze was openly admiring.

'You should always wear a lot of make-up,' he said. 'You look devastating.'

He pulled her on to the floor and guided her between the throng of dancers. All the while she kept searching for Stephen, but it was not until they had circled the floor twice and were nearing the entrance again that she saw him come in with Claire.

The girl looked devastatingly beautiful in the costume of a Spanish dancer, the slit skirt showing black silk-clad legs, the tightly laced bodice pushing up the pointed breasts. But it was at Stephen that Jane stared the longest, her very bones seeming to melt, her heart racing so fast that she could hardly breathe.

He too was dressed as a pirate, but whereas Colin looked debonair, Stephen looked a veritable buccaneer, his eyes glinting no less brightly than the ugly-looking dagger at his waist. Deeply tanned, he had not needed to darken his skin, and the one gold earring that he wore heightened his colour. A vivid red shirt, half undone, disclosed his bare chest, which seemed in the glow of electric light far more sensual than it did when he was lying by the pool in the sunlight.

'There's nothing original anywhere in the world,' Colin complained. 'Trust Stephen to pick the same as me!'

He waved, and Stephen nodded in their direction. Jane hoped they would be able to dance away from them, but she had reckoned without Claire, for the girl was determined to show off her capture, and she hailed them, making it impossible for them not to stop.

'How pretty you look, Janey,' she drawled. 'And you're wearing your jewellery after all.'

'Not without a lot of persuasion on my part,' Colin said. 'You're looking pretty nifty yourself, Claire.'

'I'd have been improved by a few of Janey's baubles. It's difficult to know what to wear with a Spanish dress.'

'Diamonds,' Colin said promptly. 'If you'd been nice to me, I'd have arranged it for you.'

The smile Claire gave him seemed false, and again Jane was concious of an undercurrent between them. Could Claire be Colin's Queen of Sheba? If so, it would account for his coming on the cruise. Yet it was obvious that Claire did not return his feelings, for though she had avowed her determination to find a husband, she did not include Colin in her calculations. 'But she's certainly included Stephen,' Jane thought as Claire moved her shoulder closer to the man at her side.

Throughout the conversation between Colin and Claire, Stephen had not once looked in Jane's direction, and it was only as the tempo of the music changed and Claire turned in his arms that he gave Jane a brief smile before turning his back to her.

With an effort she danced and joked and drank champagne, trying to pretend she did not care that Stephen was not with her. The music grew louder, the lights grew brighter and her head began to throb so that the quietness of her cabin and sleep became necessities she could no longer do without.

'I can't keep awake any longer, Colin,' she said finally. 'It's nearly two o'clock and I'm absolutely dead.'

'One more dance,' he said, 'and then I'll take you down.'

With a sigh she followed him on to the floor again, dismayed when the orchestra swung into a polka. Around the floor they whirled, jostling against other dancers, apologizing and whirling away again to bang into yet another couple. With a final crescendo the music ended and she stopped, the room revolving.

'That really was the last dance. I'm so tired I—'

The words died away and her eyes dilated. Beneath her fingers she felt the muscles of her throat contract, the skin damp to her touch.

'What's wrong, Janey? You're as white as a ghost.'

'My ruby necklace! It's gone.' She took her hand away and Colin stared at her.

'You must have dropped it.'

'I'd have heard it fall. It's far too heavy to drop un-noticed.'

'You wouldn't have heard it in all this noise. Hang on and I'll ask the orchestra leader to make an announcement.'

Jane remained where she was, trembling too much to move, while Colin walked over to the dais and whispered to the man standing on it. At once he announced the loss of the necklace over the microphone, and after a moment of heavy silence everyone stood up and began to look about them. Slowly the seconds passed, each one a heartbeat of fear for Jane, but as they ticked away into minutes the rubies were not found and her fear increased.

'It's got to be here somewhere,' she cried, and began to search the floor herself.

'Take it easy, Janey.' Colin was at her side. 'It can't be far away. Come over to the table and have a drink.'

'But I've got to find it. You don't understand, Colin. I've got to find it.'

His look was puzzled, but he caught her arm and led her over to the table. As she sank into her chair Stephen materialized in front of her, and though there was no warmth in his face the coldness had gone from it.

'The necklace must be in the ballroom,' he said quietly. 'Don't be so upset.'

'But it's worth a fortune,' she gasped.

'I'm sure it is. And I'm equally sure your father's insured it.'

With an effort she remembered who she was supposed to be and tried to muster her composure.

'If the necklace isn't recovered you've no idea how angry Dad'll be, insured or not.'

'I'm certain you'll find it.'

'But say it's been stolen!'

Her words had the effect of a bombshell and both men stared at her. Stephen's face paled and it was left to Colin to speak first.

'Don't let Dinky hear you say such a thing. He'd have a fit!'

She did not reply. Quite a few of the people on board would have a fit if they knew that one of their number was a much-sought-after thief!

'I think Jane needs a drink,' Stephen said.

Colin tried to attract the attention of a waiter, but the loss of the necklace had distracted everyone and he walked over to the bar himself.

'When did you last notice you were wearing it?' Stephen asked.

'I don't remember. It was only at the end of the waltz that I realized it had gone. I thought it had dropped off while I was whirling round.'

'If it did then it's quite likely to have been flung some distance away. There's a chance some of the people went out to get a breath of air before the orchestra leader announced the loss of your necklace . . .'

Leaving his words unfinished, he strode to the nearest door and disappeared.

Left alone, Jane twisted her hands nervously, formulating in her mind what she would say to Janey and Cedric Belton if the rubies were not found. How awful if they suspected her!

'I wish to heaven I'd never let Colin persuade me to wear the beastly things. If I ever get the necklace back I'll never wear any of them again. I'll lock them up in the Purser's office and—'

Her thoughts stopped abruptly as Stephen came through the door, triumph in his face, in his hand a glittering coil of ruby fire.

'Where did you find it?' she gasped.

'Where I thought I would. It had been flung off while you

were dancing and fell on to another woman's dress. I walked along the deck looking at all the passengers and saw some old dowager by the rails. She was wearing a bunched-up thing of net and I took a chance and asked her to turn round. Your necklace was half hidden in one of the folds of material.' He held it out to her. 'Lean forward and I'll put it on.'

She obeyed, and the necklace slithered around her neck. But she was not conscious of the cold touch of the jewels on her skin, but of the warmth of his fingers as they manoeuvred the clasp. He too was not unaware of her proximity, and she could have sworn that the tempo of his breathing changed. Yet when he stepped back and she looked into his face his expression was as inscrutable as ever.

'I'll tell the band leader to announce that you've recovered it,' he said, and walked away.

As he left, Colin returned with a couple of drinks, and Jane gulped hers down, intent on going to her cabin, taking off all the jewellery and giving it into the Purser's charge.

Colin accompanied her to the cabin and outside the door put his arm over her shoulder.

'You look so lovely, Janey. I'm sorry you had such a fright over the rubies. You're a silly girl to have got so upset. Even if the whole lot was pinched it's the insurance company that has to worry, not you.'

'I don't want *anyone* to worry,' she retorted. 'I'm giving the whole lot back to the Purser right now!'

'What's the point in having the stuff if you don't wear it?'

'It's my jewellery. I can do what I like with it.'

'I know that, old girl. It just seems a pity, that's all. Come on, then. If you're going to the Purser I might as well go with you. Otherwise you'll be afraid someone will make a grab at you while you're walking along the corridor!'

Since this was precisely what she had been thinking, she laughed nervously. 'Hang on a second while I get the rest of the stuff.'

She ran into her cabin and picked up the jewel-case from the dressing-table, taking off the jewellery she was wearing and placing it carefully inside. Holding the case in her hands as though it were a bomb, she went with Colin to the Purser's office, stopping in dismay as she saw that the wooden shutter was down and no light burned within.

Colin looked at his watch. 'It was stupid of me not to have realized. The poor chap's fast asleep. You'd better come back in the morning.'

'I can't. I won't be able to go to sleep unless I know they're safe.'

'For heaven's sake! No one's going to pinch them. You can't really be worried.'

'Is anything wrong?' a quiet voice asked, and Jane swung round to see Stephen at the foot of the stairs leading from the main deck.

'I wanted to give the Purser my jewel-case, but the office is closed.'

Stephen looked at her, and seeing her white face he walked over to a telephone placed in a niche on one of the walls and picked it up. She was too far away to hear what he said, but when he replaced the receiver he was smiling.

'The Purser will be here in a couple of moments,' he told her.

Soon footsteps were heard, and the Purser, clad in a flannel dressing-gown, his face flushed from sleep, came into sight. He took the case from her and beckoned her to come into his office, where he locked the case away in a wall safe and handed her the key.

'You'd better guard that too,' Colin grinned as she came out. 'Otherwise our famous thief will be pinching it from under the Purser's nose!'

It was a joke at which Jane could not laugh, and she put the key in her bag and held it tightly.

'You've all been very kind to me, but now if you'll excuse me, I must go to bed, I'm absolutely dead.'

Not waiting for a reply, she half ran down the corridor.

Outside her cabin she fumbled with the lock, her eyes filled with tears of relief and exhaustion.

'Here. let me do it for you.'

Shock made her motionless and without a word she gave Stephen the key and watched him manipulate the lock and open the door.

'It's silly of me not to be able to do it,' she said huskily.

'It's bent, I think. Get the steward to have a look at it in the morning.'

'I will.'

He half moved towards her and then drew back. 'Poor Jane, you really do take things to heart,' he murmured.

'So would you in my position,' she blurted out.

There was a curious puzzlement in his eyes and his mouth moved as though he were going to speak. But he seemed to think better of it and instead touched her cheek. In the rosy light that filtered down the corridor he looked taller and darker than ever, his face in shadow, only his eyes glittering and the dagger that flashed at his waist.

'Goodnight, Stephen,' she said, and unable to bear his proximity any longer, closed the door behind her.

CHAPTER NINE

FOR the next few days the *Cambrian* sailed slowly down the western coast of Italy and then up the Adriatic towards Venice. The weather was perfect, blue skies, blazing sun and cool breezes, while the evenings were star-filled and meant for love.

But Jane, spending a great deal of her time with Colin, wished she were free to leave the ship and return to England. Indeed, had it not been for the promise she had made to her father, she would have made some excuse and asked Dinky to stop at one of the small ports lining the route.

She made a second attempt to have things out with Stephen, but he had refused to listen to her and pride forbade from trying again. If he could be so jealous over such a trivial incident, she told herself angrily, then he was not worth bothering about.

Unfortunately he was still the most likely suspect, and though she had dismissed the idea that he might have stolen the jewels for money, she was almost convinced he had stolen them for the pleasure of possession.

Her reasons for thinking this had crystallized the day after they had visited Monte Carlo. They had been sitting together by the swimming-pool, for Stephen was too sophisticated to let anyone guess at his change of attitude towards her, and still maintained a friendliness, albeit on the surface.

Everyone had been discussing the theft of five priceless paintings from a gallery in Paris, avidly agreeing that though it was a daring deed, it was also a stupid one, since the pictures were too well known ever to be sold.

'Maybe the thieves will hold the insurance company up to ransom,' Claire suggested.

'They'd only get chicken feed,' Colin answered. 'The

whole thing's crazy.'

'I don't see why,' Stephen said. 'Firstly, what right do we have to assume that the paintings were stolen in order to be sold again and even to be returned? Maybe they're wanted by a collector who has a fancy for modern paintings.'

'Then he'd have to keep them hidden in his cellar,' Jane retorted. 'He'd never dare show them to a soul.'

'He mightn't want to, as long as he could see them himself. He probably gets more satisfaction out of gloating over them in private.'

'A pretty expensive price to pay for the pleasure of gloating!'

'Not if he has the money.'

Jane's mind kept returning to this conversation, and she would have given a great deal to have had free access to Stephen's home. Even if she did not learn anything else on the cruise, she was in duty bound to tell her father what little she knew and allow him to judge for himself what steps to take. Not that it would be easy to take any action against a man like Stephen. One needed more than suspicion before accusing a newspaper proprietor!

The leisurely days were enlivened by one further topic of conversation – the series of articles in the *Morning Star* disclosing the happenings on the *Cambrian*. Dinky Howard, obtaining sight of the first one when they had docked at Monte Carlo, had immediately asked Stephen if he knew anything about it, receiving the terse reply that he had had nothing to do with it whatever. But as the ship ploughed the blue waters of the Adriatic, Dinky's demeanour became more and more despondent, and it was not until one afternoon as they were all getting the last rays of the setting sun that he again talked to Stephen about it.

'Five more articles have appeared, Mr. Drake. One every day this week.'

'I didn't know you'd been getting copies of the *Morning Star*,' Stephen said to the American.

'My London office have been cabling me about it. It really

is a most *unfortunate* coincidence that it happens to be *your* paper.'

'I don't run it. I leave that to my editor.'

'Yes, but policy—'

'Policy is something I settle at our annual meeting. These sort of articles are just day-to-day bread and butter.'

'And jam too,' Dinky answered. 'Nasty, slanderous, sticky jam!'

'They're not a bit slanderous,' Jane blurted out. 'I read the first one and found it great fun. I don't know why you object to them.'

'Because my passengers pay for privacy and they're not getting it.'

'Most of your passengers adore publicity. I'm sure none of them would mind appearing in any of these articles. Why don't you ask them?'

'I don't need to ask them, Miss Belton. I—'

'Well, ask me, then!' Jane grinned. 'After all, I'm one of the passengers. And I can tell you I'll be absolutely livid if this mysterious writer doesn't include *me!*'

It was a discomfited Dinky who walked away, and Stephen gave her a frosty smile.

'There was no need to rush to my defence.'

'I'm sorry. I just didn't see why he should blame you.'

He shrugged. 'It doesn't matter to me. I just think Frank Preston should have told me what he was up to.'

'You might have stopped him!'

'You're darned right, I would! I don't like being involved in my own schemes!' He suddenly grinned. 'Perhaps Rupert's trying to earn an honest penny?'

'I doubt it,' Jane said hastily. 'The first one was written while he was still in Monte Carlo.'

'So it was. Anyway, I'm going to cable Frank to drop the whole thing. It's too embarrassing to have it go on.' He closed his eyes and turned his face up to the sun, signifying that the conversation was at an end.

The night before they were due to arrive at Venice Dinky

announced that they would not have any special excursions ashore, since he was certain that everyone would rather make their own plans.

At seven-thirty the next morning Jane was up and dressed, standing on deck as they glided slowly towards the Grand Canal. Ahead lay Venice, one of the most remarkable cities in the world. But not all the articles she had read about it or the descriptions she had heard in any way prepared her for the heart-stirring beauty of age-old buildings rising from olive-green waters. The ship ploughed past innumerable little islands, so small that they appeared to be mere outcrops of rocks on which stood an isolated house or a grove of trees. But gradually the city itself unfolded before her, and Gothic and Renaissance palaces and churches stood outlined against the sky. She was able to catch a glimpse of the church of St. Mark and the Doge's Palace, the latter bordering the Canal itself and appearing so beautiful in the shimmering light that she could hardly believe it was real.

Promptly at nine-thirty Jane descended the gangplank to the docks and, quickly cleared by the Customs officers, set out on her explorations. Her first necessity was a guide book, and she procured one at the railway station, a huge marble structure resembling a palace. With the book in her hand she made her plan for the day: museums and art galleries in the morning, lunch at one of the small restaurants she had heard so much about and then the Doge's Palace and the Basilica of St. Mark, followed by a walk through the shopping centre. How often she had laughed at the American tourists she had seen plodding through London, guide books in their hands. Now she was doing the same thing, though her desire to explore was heightened by her determination not even to admit to herself that she was upset not to be with Stephen.

As the hours passed, the streets became more crowded and the Grand Canal as busy a thoroughfare as Regent Street. Hundreds of gondolas glided up and down its length, and the air was broken by the hooters of the water buses as they ploughed their way around the city. Her guide book told her there were one hundred and seventy canals spanned by more than four hundred bridges, and by lunch-time Jane felt as though she had walked over most of them. Footsore, she plodded down one more narrow cobbled street, breathing a sigh of relief as ahead of her she saw a small restaurant from which came the appetizing smell of fish. In the window stood plates heaped with succulent-looking lobsters, golden potato crisps and crunchy, freshly friend scampi that made her mouth water. The little restaurant – in fact, café was more appropriate a word – was crammed with people, most of them eating beside a narrow counter that lined the far wall. Hesitantly she entered, wondering whether her smattering of Italian would be enough. But she need not have worried, for the woman behind the counter guessed she was a foreigner and spoke to her immediately in English. Within a moment Jane was led out to the back of the restaurant where half a dozen tables were set against a grey stone wall, shaded from the sun by a gnarled tree. A young boy played a guitar in one corner and sang incomprehensible songs in a plaintive voice, unconcerned that the chattering, hungry people around him did not hear a word.

Jane eased off her shoes beneath the table and wriggled her toes with relief, enjoying the luxury of simple food beautifully cooked. Only now did she realize how tired she was of the elaborate menus served on board the *Cambrian*.

Lunch over, she wandered towards the Piazza San Marco and approaching it from the direction of the Opera House, was given a wonderful view of the church. Had this church been set against the dreariest background it would still have seemed a thing of beauty, but set as it was against a clear blue sky and at the end of one of the most magnificent squares in the world, it was a sight to cause even the most blasé travellers to pause in appreciation.

Jane spent a long time in the church itself, admiring the mosaics on the walls and the interior arches which were covered with rare marbles. The High Altar, with its hand-worked gold and silver, was one of the chief glories, and she stood for a long while in front of it. Difficult to believe that human hands could have made it, so intricate was its design, so exact its composition.

When she came out into the bright sunlight, she stood for a moment blinking until her eyes had become accustomed to the glare, and as she paused felt a flutter of wings against her hair. The pigeons of the Piazza San Marco, like the pigeons of Trafalgar Square, gave life and noise to their surroundings, and the constant flutter of wings was like the rustle of leaves, becoming so loud at times it was as though they were moved by a gale! Never had she seen so many pigeons – in their thousands, indeed in their hundreds of thousands they swooped and swerved, fluttered and flew around her, coming to rest at her feet where they pecked the ground for a moment before returning to the high arches they had made their home.

There were so many tourists in the Piazza, mostly American, that it was difficult to spot an Italian, but these could usually be discerned by the nonchalant way they walked past the magnificent shops and never once glanced at the church or the tall, brick-built bell-tower that stood in front of it.

From the top of this tower one would be able to get an extensive view of the city, and as soon as she had finished her coffee she walked across to it, paid her money and was wafted in a lift to the very top.

For a long time she stood looking down at the houses and palaces, so intent on the panorama that she was unaware of the hands of the clock creeping round to four. There was a faint whirring in the air and then a roar so loud that it vibrated in her eardrums, throbbing and beating and seeming to shatter her very soul. With a gasp of pain she covered her ears, her body reeling as the huge bells above her head clanged back and forth.

Suddenly firm hands caught her round the waist, steadying her, and she remained leaning in their circle until the last vibration faded away. Only then did she turn and look into Stephen's dark, well-beloved face.

'Did no one warn you about the bells?' he asked calmly.

She shook her head, unable to speak, and putting his hand beneath her elbow he guided her to the lift and pressed the button.

'It's a pretty shattering experience to hear them at such close quarters,' he said. 'And of course if it happens without any warning . . .'

'I thought I was going to faint,' she admitted. 'It was silly of me, I know, but—'

'Some people are more allergic to noise than others. Personally, noise doesn't worry me, though I can't stand a knife grinding on a plate!'

The lift doors opened and they stepped in.

'You're the last person I expected to see here,' she murmured. 'I'd have thought you'd have seen the Campanile before.'

'I have. Many times. But whenever I come to Venice I always like to look at the city again.'

'It's beautiful, isn't it?'

'Yes. I prefer it to Rome.'

The lift doors opened and they walked down the steps and into the Piazza. Stephen hesitated, and Jane knew she should take the initiative and leave, but she could not move, could not bear to go away from him.

'I'm surprised Colin didn't go up the tower with you,' he said.

'Why should he?'

'*I* wouldn't have let you go alone.'

'But I *am* alone. Colin isn't with me – he's at the Lido.'

She turned and walked swiftly across the Square, head high, eyes blinking rapidly to prevent the falling of the tears that blurred her vision.

'Jane, wait!'

Afraid she had imagined her name called, she continued

to walk, only stopping as Stephen spoke directly behind her.

'Let me buy you a coffee,' he said. 'I'm sure you can do with it.'

He escorted her to a table and a waiter came up to them at once. Stephen gave their order and then leaned back in his chair and looked at her. Happiness rose within her, died away and then rose once more. She and Stephen were together again. Why question it? Why not accept the pleasure for what it was worth . . .? But what *was* it worth? To have him be nice to her for a few moments and then walk away was more than she could bear. At the risk of another rebuff, she must try and talk to him intimately.

'You've a habit of pairing me off with other men, haven't you?' She marvelled that her voice could sound so calm. 'First it was Rupert and now it's Colin.'

'You can't blame me. You're a high-spirited girl and I don't suppose you realize how things can be misinterpreted.'

'I don't see how anyone could misinterpret my having a drink with Rupert,' she said flatly.

'And what about Colin? How is one supposed to regard a secret engagement?'

'A secret engagement? I don't know what you're talking about.'

'I'm sorry if I'm not supposed to know,' he said stiffly, 'but you shouldn't confide in Rupert.'

'Oh, lord!' Jane said. 'You don't mean you believed what he told you? I made it up! I couldn't bear having him under my feet for the rest of the cruise, so I implied that Colin and I were in love. I'd have used *you* instead of Colin if you hadn't made it so obvious you couldn't stand the sight of me.'

He made no comment, and she busied herself with the coffee pot, stirring her cup long after the sugar had dissolved. Behind them a small orchestra played romantic Stauss waltzes and above them pigeons wheeled, dark feathery shapes in the bright sky.

A couple more fluttered at their feet; a male hopped around a female, puffing out his chest and waving his wings to attract her attention. His efforts came to naught, for she pecked at him and flew away and, after pausing for a few seconds, he strutted over to another female and began to repeat the dance.

'They never take no for an answer,' Stephen said dryly. 'I guess they haven't any pride.'

'A good thing too. Pride and jealousy cause far too much unhappiness.'

'I gather from that,' he said dryly, 'that you think I should emulate the pigeons! Well, maybe you're right. I realize I've been behaving stupidly the last few days.'

She longed to deny what he had said, but the words would not come, for she was so happy to know he wanted to be friends again that she was too moved to speak. Her silence served her in good stead, for he leaned forward and caught her hand.

'I'm sorry for behaving the way I did, Jane. I've no excuse to make except that I'm not a pigeon!'

She burst out laughing. 'I never thought you were. A hawk or an eagle, perhaps, but never a pigeon!'

It was his turn to laugh. 'You're such fun to be with. Your father must miss you when you're away.'

'He does. He's not had an easy life since my mother died and I like to be with him as much as I can.'

'You're fond of him, aren't you?'

'Yes.' She did not continue, for she saw a brooding look on his face, a look she had seen many times before.

'I never had any feelings for *my* father,' he said unexpectedly. 'He never loved my mother, and I hated him for it!'

There was so much Jane wanted to say that she did not know how to begin and, afraid lest she say the wrong thing, she chose her words with care.

'You can't hate a person because they don't love someone, even if that someone was your mother.'

'I know that now, but when you're a youngster you don't

see things in the same way. I didn't understand how anyone could live with my mother and *not* love her. I didn't understand why my father preferred all those – all those other women. Yet she went on loving him – my mother, I mean – and even now she won't hear a word against him.'

'How does she excuse him?' Jane asked.

'She doesn't. You see, she never blamed my father because he didn't love her. From that you'll gather that my mother's a very humble woman – not a bit like me!' He took a cigarette from his case and lit it. 'I could never bear to be in the position she was. From the time I was old enough to understand I vowed I wouldn't allow myself to be hurt, wouldn't allow another person to make my life a torment.'

'What about your fiancée?'

'My one mistake. After it was over I vowed I'd never fall in love again.'

'I don't think you've been in love at all,' she said bluntly. 'And I think that's one of the reasons your engagement ended. I don't know Georgina, so I'm not trying to excuse her, but believe me, if a woman thinks she loves a man more than he loves her, she'll do everything in her power to make him prove her wrong.'

'By trying to take over his business? Georgina would only have been happy if she could have controlled everything I did.'

'Maybe she thought it was the only way she could be a part of your life.'

He was so long answering that she did not think he was going to do so. But eventually he spoke, his voice so low that she had the impression he was speaking more to himself.

'I wonder if you're right. If you are, it would explain a lot of things ... Still, it's over now. What I felt for her is dead.'

'One day there'll be someone else,' she whispered. 'That's the time you must remember that if you want to be loved you mustn't be afraid of loving.'

'I'm not afraid.'

'Of course you are. You've already admitted it. You're afraid of being like your mother!'

He sighed. 'If two people love one another there should be sufficient understanding to—'

'Understanding's got nothing to do with love! You can fall in love with someone at first sight, but that doesn't mean you *understand* them. That takes time, sometimes years. Honestly, Stephen, for a man of thirty-five you talk like a baby.'

He moved irritably. 'You're only a baby yourself.'

'It's silly of you to keep bringing up my age,' she retorted. 'It's probably another one of your defence mechanisms. If you say I'm a child often enough you might begin to believe it!'

'How do you know I don't?'

'You didn't kiss me as if I were a child.' The words were out before she could stop them and her cheeks burned with embarrassment. As he saw it, his good humour returned.

'You didn't respond like a child either, if I may say so. In fact, very much to the contrary.'

He crossed his legs and looked intently at his shoe, as though what he was going to say was written on it.

'When I first met you I thought of you as a child. An amusing one but a child nonetheless. I also thought that your presence would prevent me from having to ward off the attentions of other charming but certainly less childish women.'

The angry retort that hovered on her lips was never uttered, for he held up his hand.

'No, Jane, let me finish. After we spent that day in Cannes I revised my opinions. You're years younger than I am, but ... there's something about you ... You're so wise. So oddly wise.' He looked up, his face disclosing an emotion he had only once before displayed to her. 'We seem to choose our times badly. I wish to hell we were alone!'

He dropped some coins on the table and stood up. 'I must talk to you tonight. After dinner we'll go off by ourselves. Is that all right with you?'

'Yes,' she said, and gave him her hand. 'Oh, Stephen, yes.'

For the next few hours Stephen showed Jane the parts of Venice she had not known existed. Tiny museums which, though they did not house the magnificent paintings and relics of the larger ones, nonetheless gave her a more intimate picture of the past. As she stared at frayed, brocade-covered furniture in dusty salons where once young women and men had danced to the flute and the harp, she was able to see a clearer picture of the Venice of the past than she had done when walking through the glittering and well-preserved *palazzos*. But no matter where they went there was always the dark green water around them, the swish of the paddle and the mournful cry of the gondolier as he swung his boat around the winding canals.

In the main thoroughfares the chatter of people and the sound of laughter was a constant background, yet in the inner regions of the city there was a magic quiet. It vested the most ordinary things with unexpected beauty, enabling one to slip easily back into the past and to savour it as though it were the present. But even tranquillity had to come to an end, and the stars were twinkling in the sky as they glided in a gondola down the Grand Canal back to the bustle and lights of the Danielli Hotel.

'Will you want to go back to the boat to change?' Stephen asked her.

'I don't think so. I promised to have a drink with Colin first.'

'What a pity. I'll be glad to get you back to London, Jane. It's hard getting to know someone in a strange country. You get dazzled by false rumour.'

'There's nothing very glamorous about me at the moment,' she laughed. 'I haven't had a wash all day and I feel dirty and shiny.'

'You look lovely,' he said, and leaning forward, kissed her nose.

'Oh, Stephen, it's so funny, your doing that. I never thought the owner of the *Morning Star* would—' She stopped, confused, but he only laughed.

'I never thought I'd be kissing Belton's Bakeries, either!'

Their gondola swung round to the side entrance of the Danielli and a porter helped her out and up the steps into the lobby. Facing her was a magnificent flowering tree, its cyclamen-coloured blossoms soaring high into the air. Together she and Stephen walked across the marble floor to the bar, and they were at the door when they were hailed by a grey-haired woman in fluttery blue silk.

'Why, Stephen, what a surprise to see you here! Your mother said you were due in Venice, but she wasn't sure when!'

'Mrs. Martin! How good to see you.'

Stephen kissed her on the cheek and as he drew back the woman looked in Jane's direction.

'I'd like you to meet Janey Belton,' he said smoothly, 'one of my fellow passengers.'

Jane held out her hand, and Mrs. Martin took it, holding it a fraction longer than necessary.

'Janey Belton?' She stressed the name. 'Are you related to Cedric Belton?'

'He's my – my father.'

'Your father!' Mrs. Martin peered into her bag and fumbled for a handkerchief. At that moment Claire and Colin came in through the main door of the hotel and, seeing them at the other end of the lobby, waved a greeting.

'I didn't know Claire was on the boat too,' Mrs. Martin said, and greeted the girl with great warmth. It was a warmth fully returned, and Jane could not help waspishly assuming that Mrs. Martin must be rich and well-connected. Claire would not bother with a woman otherwise.

'What about us all having a drink?' Stephen suggested. 'It's more comfortable at the bar than out here.'

'You go without me,' Mrs. Martin said. 'I've got some

letters to write. Though perhaps Claire would like to come upstairs and have a wash in my room?'

Jane was surprised at the question, for Claire was dressed for the evening and it was obvious she had returned to the boat to change.

'Do come up for a moment,' Mrs. Martin reiterated, and caught hold of Claire's arm.

There was more than normal pressure in the grasp, for the fingers paled and Jane was certain that something lay beneath the suggestion. Claire must have felt so too, for with a smile she allowed the woman to lead her to the lift.

Stephen waited until they had disappeared and then entered the bar. It was crowded and noisy, an orchestra adding to the babel.

'Let's make it a quick one,' he said. 'I won't be able to stand this place for long.'

As he turned to give their order to the waiter Colin looked at Jane and raised his eyebrows. She nodded imperceptibly and he smiled.

They were having a second drink when Claire returned, and as she reached their table Jane saw a glitter in her eyes, a smile of triumph on her lips.

'We'd nearly given you up,' Stephen said. 'I took a chance and ordered you champagne.'

'Not much of a chance, darling. I'm always ready for that.'

She sat down and accepted a cigarette from Colin. Her hand were shaking and Jane was certain that Mrs. Martin had told her something to upset her. Yet she did not look upset. On the contrary, she looked exceptionally pleased.

'Do you want to change to champagne too, Jane?' Stephen asked.

'No, thanks. I'll stick to orange juice.'

'Don't tell me you're refusing champagne,' Claire drawled. 'I should have thought you'd have jumped at the opportunity.'

Stephen and Colin looked surprised at the unexpected

cattiness of the remark, but Jane determined to pretend she was unaware of it.

'I don't like changing my drinks,' she said lightly.

'You're not so scrupulous when it comes to changing your name, are you?'

This time Jane could not pretend. Her mouth went dry and she set her glass on the table, spilling a little liquid.

'You can't find an answer to that, can you, Janey?' Claire continued. 'Do forgive me calling you Janey, but I'm afraid I don't know your real name!'

CHAPTER TEN

AFTER Claire's dramatic statement there was no sound at the table. It served to emphasize the noise around them, making Jane feel as though she were trapped in an oasis of silence.

'What on earth are you talking about?' Stephen asked at last. 'Is this a joke, Claire?'

'If it is then the joke's on us! Mrs. Martin asked me up to her room in order to tell me that she happens to know Janey Belton – and she certainly isn't the little impostor who's with us now!'

Jane's throat contracted, but words would not come.

'Is this true?' Stephen asked her.

Courage came back to Jane and with it her voice. 'Yes. But I can explain.'

'I should hope so,' Claire drawled. 'And I bet it's a pretty good story, too. What have you done with the real Janey – kidnapped her?'

Ignoring the question, Jane looked at the two men. 'Janey Belton *asked* me to take her place because she had reasons for wanting to stay in England.'

'Who are you, then? What's your real name?' There was no expression on Stephen's face and she had no means of knowing what he felt about her disclosure.

'I'm Jane Berry.'

'So it *is* Jane.' He smiled. 'I knew Janey didn't suit you.'

Claire looked at the two of them, anger visible as she saw that Stephen did not appear to be annoyed at the impersonation.

'I don't see why you couldn't have let us in on the secret,' she said spitefully. 'Once you were miles away from England Cedric Belton couldn't have done anything about it.'

'It wasn't my secret to tell.'

'Surely you could have told *Stephen* . . .'

Jane bit her lip. Had she been an ordinary girl, a friend of Janey's, she would certainly have done so. But she was not a friend of Janey's; she was a working girl and, most difficult of all, she had fallen in love with her boss!

'Well, now we do know who you are,' Colin said, 'let's forget the whole thing.' He picked up his glass. 'I don't know about anyone else, but I think we should toast Jane Belton, alias Jane—' He hesitated. 'Berry, did you say?'

She nodded, and Claire looked at her with curiosity. 'I take it you're a friend of Janey's?'

'Yes.'

'Are you the same age?'

'I'm twenty-three.'

'You're not one of her contemporaries, then? I must say you gave a very good impersonation.' Claire's eyes narrowed. 'You really did have us fooled. What do you do?'

'What do I do?'

Jane tried to prevaricate. Although she could not tell Stephen the *real* purpose of her trip, she had every intention of telling him that she worked on his paper; but she wanted to do it in her own time and when they were alone.

'Yes,' Claire repeated. 'What do you do?'

'*I* can answer *that* question,' Dinky Howard said, suddenly materializing before them. His pink face was red with indignation and his claw-like hands fluttered across his stomach. 'It just so happens I've been speaking to my London office and they told me Cedric Belton rang them because he's just discovered his daughter is not on board and that her place was taken by a *newspaper* reporter!' Dinky's voice rose. '*Your* newspaper, Mr. Drake!'

Stephen banged his glass down on the table and looked at Jane. 'Is this true?'

'Yes. I – I work on the Features page.'

Claire's laughter rippled through the horrified silence. 'So that's why you impersonated Janey. There's nothing a reporter won't do for a story!'

'I didn't ask to do it,' Jane said. 'Janey Belton asked *me*.'

'I don't care who asked whom,' Dinky squeaked. 'All I'm concerned with is that you came on board to spy!'

'And find a rich husband too,' Claire drawled. 'Not that I blame you for having a try.'

'You've no right to say that,' Jane retorted, and wished she could tell them that she had refused to go on the cruise, that she had only done so to help her father. But none of this could be said. There was still too much at stake.

'Not that I blame you,' Claire repeated. 'After all, a millionaire's cruise is a working girl's dream.'

'Cut it out, Claire,' Colin said. 'Jane was only doing her job.'

'She applied herself to it with great industry.' Claire looked at Stephen. 'And there you were, thinking you were protecting an innocent little heiress while all the time she's a hard-boiled member of your own staff!'

Jane stood up. 'I've had enough,' she said huskily, and before anyone could stop her, ran from the room.

Outside the Danielli she paused and then, turning right, ran along by the side of the canal. There were scores of gondolas parked at the edge and she climbed into the first one and told him to go to the ship.

Fate could not have behaved more cruelly to her. Stephen only knew half the story and because of it was no doubt misjudging her as badly as Claire. Not that she could blame him. Seen at surface level her impersonation of Janey Belton had been done for the sake of a good story and possibly – how could she deny it? – the chance of finding a rich husband. Unexpectedly she remembered Edward Hawton, and his fatal accident which had not been an accident at all. She shivered and blinked away her tears.

Ahead loomed the white hulk of the *Cambrian* and the gondola glided to a stop in front of some stone steps. She paid the man, and climbing out, walked the length of the quay to the gangplank. It was quiet on board the ship and she realized that most of the passengers were dining ashore. In the normal course of events she would have left the ship and returned home; but these were not normal circumstances. Her father was certain the thief would try and get the Lorenz Diamond re-cut in Athens, and she was determined to remain on board until they docked there.

Dejectedly she went to her cabin and, flinging herself on the bed, gave way to tears. No longer was she a hard-boiled member of Stephen's staff, but the heartbroken woman who loved him.

After a long while she sat up and wiped her eyes. Her face was puffy from crying, and going into the bathroom she splashed her eyes with cold water. She was sitting at the dressing-table combing her hair when there was a knock at the door and her heart leaped in panic.

'Who is it?'

'Stephen. I want to see you.'

She opened the door and he stepped inside. Beneath his tan he was deathly pale, the familiar vein beating at the side of his cheek, a sure sign of tension.

'You had no business to run off like that,' he said harshly.

'I wasn't going to stay and be insulted by Claire!'

He looked round the cabin. 'I assumed you were packing to leave. You surely don't intend to write any more articles?'

'Of course not.'

'Then why aren't you going?'

'Because Janey asked me to take her place and I'm entitled to stay on board for the whole journey.'

'My God, you've got a nerve!'

'I don't see why. At least I can enjoy the rest of the trip.'

'Husband-hunting, no doubt.'

'Stephen, don't! It's not fair.'

'How dare you talk about fairness?' He gripped her shoulders. 'Why didn't you tell me the truth?'

'I couldn't. It wasn't my secret.'

'Secret?' he grated. 'Why make such a big thing of the secret? Do you think Janey Belton would have cared if you'd told me your real name? Do you think it was right to let me go on believing you were someone else, to become fond of a person who didn't exist?'

'But I do exist. I'm still me!' she said passionately. 'Just because my name's different it doesn't mean *I'm* different.'

'Of course you're different. You're a reporter doing a job, and taking the opportunity of ingratiating herself with the man who employs her!'

She wrenched herself free from him. 'If you think I only came on board to get a story—'

'What else can I think!'

She said nothing, and he pulled her round to face him.

'Haven't you anything more to say to me?'

'No. You wouldn't believe me anyway.'

'You're right about that.' His voice was harsh. 'From the moment we met you lied to me. If you'd only come on board in order to get a story you'd have disclosed your identity to me before today. Damn it all, most of the articles have been printed by now, so you weren't afraid I might have stopped them appearing. But you *didn't* tell me. And the reason is because you knew I was falling for you. You were banking on finding a rich husband, and believe me, another week and you'd have succeeded!'

'I'd no such thoughts in my mind! I liked you, Stephen. I hated having to lie to you, but I—'

'But you did. And you've no excuse for it.' He dropped his hand from her arm and moved back. 'You look so innocent, yet you're a liar and a cheat!'

The door slammed behind him and Jane sank on the bed and buried her head in her hands. Never in her worst moments had she thought Stephen would be so unreasonable. Yet his very behaviour bespoke the love he had not

146

allowed himself to utter, and she took heart from this, her anger dissolving with understanding. Shakily she turned back to the mirror and picked up her hairbrush.

She was applying the finishing touches to her make-up when there was another knock at the door. Could it be Stephen come back to apologize? Quickly she applied her lipstick and ran to open it, but when she did so it was not Stephen who stepped forward, but Colin.

'Hello there. I'd like to talk to you.'

'More taunting?'

'Certainly not.' He stepped into the cabin and closed the door. 'I only want to apologize for Claire's behaviour, and also to let you know that I don't care who you really are. As far as I'm concerned you're the girl I liked from the moment we met.'

'Oh, Colin!' Tears filled her eyes. 'I couldn't have borne it if you'd called me a cheat as well.'

'Stephen, I suppose?'

She nodded, not trusting herself to speak.

'Don't judge him too harshly,' Colin said. 'I suppose he felt guilty over the whole thing. After all, you do work for him, and Dinky probably thinks you were in cahoots together.'

'We certainly weren't. Stephen had no idea who I was. If he had he wouldn't have been seen dead with me! He doesn't believe in the integrity of working girls.'

'Don't talk rot. Personally I'm glad to find out you work. You were much too intelligent just to be an heiress!'

'Can't money and brains go together?'

'They can and they do,' he assured her solemnly. 'But generally with men – rarely with women. Now come on, old girl. Put on your diamonds and I'll take you out to dinner.'

She shivered. 'No more jewellery for me. I'll never forget the night I lost that ruby necklace.'

'Ah yes.' He ran a hand over his silver-blond hair. 'I realize now why you were so upset.'

'I was scared in case the Beltons thought I'd taken it. The rich have a habit of suspecting the worst of the poor,' she said bitterly.

'No one would suspect *you*,' Colin said. 'But if you don't want to wear any jewellery I'll buy you some Venetian glass beads instead.'

She laughed and picked up her handbag. Outside her stateroom she locked the door and slipped the key into her purse.

'I bet you guard the jewel-key with your life,' he grinned.

'You can say that again! And I won't tell you where I keep it either!'

'Don't tantalize me, Jane. You're pretty enough on your own without the added lure of a key to your jewel-case!'

Colin took her to dine at an open-air restaurant opposite the Fenice Opera House, and sitting at a candle-lit table she was able to relax. Good food and wine did their work and, seeing the colour return to her cheeks, he nodded with satisfaction.

'I could slap Claire for the way she behaved,' he said. 'I've never known her to be so catty.'

'It's because of Stephen,' Jane replied. 'If he hadn't liked me she wouldn't have cared about the masquerade, but she knew it would be an ideal opportunity to part us.'

'She's succeeded, hasn't she?'

'Yes.'

'I'm sorry,' he said sympathetically. 'But maybe it's for the best. If Stephen can't overlook a little pretence . . .'

He put his elbows on the table and leaned forward. 'You know what I'd do, Jane? I'd forget your job and everything else and just enjoy yourself for the rest of the cruise. Live it up. Pretend you *are* Janey Belton! You've got her clothes, her jewellery and her name until the day you return to England, so for heaven's sake take advantage of it.'

'I couldn't. There's no point in the masquerade any more. Everyone knows who I am.'

Colin leaned back, his face in shadow, his pale eyes unusually dark.

'Don't tell me you're leaving the ship? That would be too much like giving in.'

'No, I'm not leaving.'

'Thank goodness for that. After all, you're travelling on old Belton's money, so you might as well take advantage of it.'

Jane picked up her fork and continued to eat. Colin's championing of her had been a surprise, for he was even nicer to her now he knew she was only a reporter than he had been when he had thought her an heiress! 'What a difference from Stephen,' she thought bleakly, and found herself unable to swallow the food in her mouth.

It was nearly midnight when they took a gondola back to the ship, and as they glided over the dark water she thought again of Stephen. Was he with Claire? Instinctively she knew he was, knew too that fury against herself would drive him into being too friendly, too passionate towards another woman. She clenched her hands, her nails digging deep into her palms. She must put him out of her mind; memory of him would only bring unhappiness.

'Snap out of it,' Colin said quietly. 'You're sitting there as tense as a wound-up spring.'

'I'm sorry.' With an effort she relaxed, feeling the leather damp against her skin. 'I wonder if Stephen and Claire will fall in love?'

'Claire doesn't love anyone except herself.'

'But she wants to get married, and Stephen's very eligible.'

'Claire won't marry him. You can take that from me.'

Jane looked at him. It was dark on the water and the lantern glowing on the prow of the gondola did nothing to lighten his expression, enhancing the shadows over his face, making his hair look silver. Again she was convinced that Colin loved Claire and decided it would be diplomatic not to question his remark.

It was not until she was in her cabin that tears threatened to come again, but she fought them back, refusing to give way to self-pity. She took off her dress and hung it in the wardrobe, then kicked off her shoes and looked round for her slippers. One was by the dressing-table and the other under the bed. She bent to pick it up, and as she did so her eye was caught by a glint of gold on the rose-coloured carpet. For a moment she remained immobile, then she moved closer and stared at it. It was a small coin, and she lifted it up and held it in the palm of her hand. One side was plain, and with a trembling finger she turned it over, knowing even as she did so what the other side would show: an entwined letter 'L'. The talisman her father had spoken of . . . So he had been right after all: the thief *was* on board the *Cambrian*. Not only on board, but had actually been here in her cabin.

Jane groped for a chair and sat down. In her cabin . . . When she had come back to it earlier this evening the bed had already been turned down for the night and no one had entered it since except Colin and Stephen.

Colin and Stephen. One of them had dropped it here when he had come to see her. But which one? She could not go to sleep with the question unanswered, and not giving herself time to change her mind, she put on her pink satin dressing-gown and headed down the corridor to Colin's cabin. Should she show him the coin and ask if it was his? And what would happen if he denied it? Should she then show it to Stephen? She was still undecided when she reached Colin's door and with a trembling hand knocked upon it.

He opened it almost at once, looking at her in surprise.

'Jane, is anything wrong?'

'I – I've a terrible headache and I can't find any aspirins. I rang for the steward, but no one answered.'

'They're probably on shore.' He stepped back. 'Anyway I'm glad you had the sense to come to me. I've a bottle of 'em somewhere. Come in and I'll find them for you.'

She stepped inside and closed the door, watching as he

150

peered on the dressing-table and opened and closed several drawers.

'I could have sworn I had the bottle here. But maybe it's in the bathroom.'

He walked past her and she stepped over to the dressing-table and stared unseeingly at her reflection in the mirror. Suddenly she knew what she had to do and, glancing swiftly over her shoulder to make sure Colin was out of sight, she took the coin from her pocket and dropped it on the floor. Hardly had it fallen when he came out of the bathroom, a bottle in his hand.

'Here it is.' In the act of handing it to her he stopped. 'You're not going to do anything silly, are you?'

'Silly?' She stared at him uncomprehendingly. Then she realized what he meant. 'No, I'd never do that. No man's worth it!'

He smiled. 'I'm glad to hear you say that.'

She took the bottle and put it in her pocket, lowering her head as she did so.

'What's that?' Even to herself her voice sounded false.

'What?' Colin asked.

'There! On the floor at your feet. Something's glinting.'

He looked down and then bent and picked up the coin. Jane held her breath, trying with all her willpower not to show the tenseness she felt. Seconds passed as she waited for him to speak, and heightened consciousness made her aware of every sound; the creak of timber, the whirr of air-conditioning, the hum of electric generators.

'I must have dropped it when I took off my jacket,' he said casually, and slipped the coin into his trouser pocket.

Relief flooded through Jane; her one coherent thought that it had not been Stephen after all. Hard on this knowledge came the realization that she was at last face to face with the thief. Not merely the thief, but the man responsible for the murder of Edward Hawton. Though Colin himself might not have killed the ex-jockey, the order to do so had come from him, and she shivered uncontrollably.

'Jane, you've gone white. Sit down a moment.'

'No, no, I'll be all right. It's my head. I'll go back to the cabin and lie down.' With an effort she smiled at him. 'Thanks for the aspirins. I'll return them in the morning.'

She wrenched open the door and stepped outside, pausing a moment to regain her control. As the lock clicked into place she became aware of the man at the end of the corridor. Stephen! She did not need to be near him to see the contempt in his eyes nor the scorn in the twist of his mouth. Conscious of the invidiousness of her position, she flushed, her limbs trembling as she began to walk towards him. He said nothing until she was abreast of him. Only then did he move and bar her way.

'Please let me pass.'

'I've something to say to you first.'

'You said all you needed to earlier this evening.'

'I've a bit more to add,' he answered grimly. 'When you're in England you can do what you like in your spare time, but as long as you're on this ship you're supposed to be working for the *Star*, and while you are, you've got to behave yourself!'

She went white. 'Are you suggesting—?'

'I'm suggesting nothing.' His eyes were fixed on her satin dressing-gown which outlined the curve of her breasts, making it obvious that she only wore the flimsiest garment underneath. 'I'm simply telling you that while you're working for me you must keep away from men's cabins!'

'But I'm not working for you any more.' Her voice was low and filled with anger. 'After the way you've spoken to me I wouldn't work for you if you were the last man on earth!'

Her hands came up to push him out of the way and he caught them roughly and spun her against the wall.

'Don't you hit me, you vixen! If you're going to be free and easy make sure it's with kisses – not blows!'

Before she could evade him his mouth pressed hard on her

own, his body pinning her motionless. His hands came up and cupped her face, making it impossible for her to turn away. She struggled and twisted in his grasp, but the violence of her movements only loosened her dressing-gown.

Fear washed away anger, and the misery she felt was so deep that she began to cry. Tears flowed down her cheeks, trickling against the side of her mouth, and only at the feel of their wetness did his sanity return and he drew back.

She swayed and pulled her satin skirts around her. 'I'll never forgive you for this,' she whispered. 'Never!'

'I'll never forgive myself,' he said, and turning on his heel, walked away.

CHAPTER ELEVEN

THE next three days were ones of great unhappiness for Jane, and she continually relived her last scene with Stephen. How could he have behaved like that! How dared he assume that because she had been masquerading as Janey Belton she was also a gold-digger and worse? The knowledge of how sorry he would be when he learned the truth did nothing to assuage her present misery, a misery which increased at sight of his attentiveness to Claire.

They were now sailing past the coast of Greece with Piraeus only a day's journey away. Colin had not yet suggested they spend their time in Athens together, but in all their conversations she had deliberately implied that she was expecting to do so, hoping to make it impossible for him to go off alone. Yet logic told her that if he wanted to be by himself he would have no hesitation in doing so, and she was banking on the fact that he intended to use her company as a cover.

She leaned over the rails and listened to the gentle soughing of the waves. By this time tomorrow she might already have met the man Colin had come to see, and once she had done so the rest of her task was simple: contact Mr. Aristophanes of the Greek police. The thought of it made her tremble. She might have a nose for a story, but when it came to real sleuthing she was out of her depth. No longer was she the burning suffragette but a frail female desperately wanting a male shoulder behind which to hide!

She stared out at the sea, her hands clenched on the rails. Somehow she did not feel that anything that happened would make any difference to her future with Stephen. 'Or rather, to my lack of future with him,' she thought bitterly. 'I don't belong to his world and I'll never have another chance of pretending that I do.'

At dawn the following day the *Cambrian* sailed into the harbour of Piraeus, and by the time Jane had breakfasted, her landing card was waiting for her at the Purser's office. She had arranged to meet Colin here and she looked around for him, hoping he had not given her the slip. She walked the length of the deck and was beginning to grow anxious when she saw him in the distance.

He did not see her, but walked instead towards one of the lifeboats. Instinctively, sensing something in his demeanour, she stepped out of sight, delighted that she had relied on her intuition as she saw Claire come out of a side door and go across to him.

'This is it.' Colin's voice was quiet, but Jane, hidden by a pile of deck-chairs, could hear every word. 'Are you going to change your mind, Claire?'

'No. I've told you that before.'

'You're making a mistake. Stephen won't marry you, you know, and you'll be left high and dry.'

'I'll take that chance.'

'Well, you know where to contact me if you want me.'

'Does Dinky know you're leaving the ship here?'

'I haven't told *anyone*.'

'Not even Jane?' Claire said spitefully. 'I'm surprised you don't take her with you instead of me.'

'She's a nice girl,' Colin replied, 'but I don't love her.'

'Then why have you been hanging round her ever since we left Venice?'

'It suited me,' he said curtly.

'You mean the Belton jewels suited you! I've been expecting her to rush up shrieking that they've been stolen.'

Colin's laugh, though light, was unpleasant. 'Sometimes you're too melodramatic, my dear. I admit the jewels were a great temptation and at one time I did consider helping myself to them. But after due thought I realize it would be stupid to take such a risk.'

'I've never known you worry about a risk before. The bigger the danger the more you liked it. Oh, Colin,' there was unexpected pleading in Claire's voice, 'if only you'd been content with what you had. If only—'

'If only *I'd* been content!' His voice rose and he looked round him quickly. Jane, afraid to breathe, drew as far back as she could, and Colin, seeing nothing, turned to Claire again. 'You're the one who was never satisfied. How many years ago did I ask you to marry me? Six, seven? But no, I didn't have enough to keep you in the state to which you'd never been accustomed. It was for you I—'

'Oh, not that again,' Claire said wearily. 'Don't blame *me* because you turned into a thief! You'd have done the same whether I married you or not. You wanted money and you didn't want to work for it. Instead you pinched it from your friends.'

There was the scraping of a match and a pause.

'Anyway, there's no point in all this,' Claire continued. 'I'm not going with you, and that's final.'

'Very well. But if you do change your mind . . .'

There was no answer, only the clatter of high heels growing fainter in the distance.

Jane moved cautiously, but the smell of cigarette smoke made her stiffen into immobility again and she waited, palms damp, until she heard Colin move away. Quickly she came out of hiding and began to saunter down the deck. Colin was at the far end and she called him and waved.

'Sorry I'm late, Colin.'

'That's all right. I've only just got here.' He came forward. 'You look very pretty this morning.'

With his hand under her elbow they walked across the wide quay and through the Customs Hall to the other side, where taxis and guides were waiting.

'What are we going to do?' she asked. 'I hear Astia Beach is lovely.'

'You don't want any more sunbathing. The thing to do now is to visit the Acropolis.'

'And afterwards?'

'Afterwards—' There was hesitation in his voice and she

was certain he had not planned on any afterwards, that he had only thought in terms of the Acropolis. That meant he was going to meet his accomplice there! Among hosts of sightseers it would be easy to pass over the diamond and to arrange another meeting, by which time the stone would be cut. She must warn the police at once. But how? She racked her brains, wondering what to do.

'Look!' Colin said. 'Up there on the hill.'

Jane stared out of the window. Far head, above the misty panorama of the distant city, marble columns rose to the sky, and even in this scene of light and sunshine they had a radiance of their own.

'How beautiful they are. They seem to shimmer.'

He nodded. 'They're just as beautiful when you see them close up. We'll be there in about fifteen minutes.'

'Isn't it too early to go?'

He laughed. 'It's never too early to visit the Acropolis. It's always crowded.'

This was an understatement, Jane decided a little while later, as they left their taxi behind and climbed the steps leading to the most famous ruins in the world. Everywhere people swarmed and French, German and English voices shattered the air.

Unfortunately Jane was afraid to concentrate on anything except the man at her side, and watching him, she saw he was anxiously scanning the crowds. She had formulated some sort of plan, and though not sure it would work, was determined to take a chance. The first thing was to give a hint, and she stopped walking and swayed.

Colin looked at her. 'Not tired already?'

'No, just a bit giddy. I get migraine and I've an awful feeling it's coming on now.'

'I hope not.' Colin peered into her eyes. 'Let's go up to the top and you can sit down and rest.'

'Can't we go to a hotel? Or back to the boat?'

'It's too far. Come on, Jane, it's cooler higher up and I'm sure you'll feel better.'

Convinced that the person he was due to meet would be waiting for him at the summit, Jane let him lead her the rest of the way, not pausing until they reached the beautifully sculptured caryatids which supported the temple of the Erechtheum.

'There are some rocks over here you can sit on.' Colin pushed her down and she half closed her eyes.

'Don't leave me. I feel awful.'

'Of course I won't leave you.' He glanced round as he spoke and she was aware that his body had stiffened. Turning her head, she saw a swarthy man in a creased fawn suit walking purposefully in their direction. Before he could reach them she stood up and leaned heavily against Colin.

'I can't stay here. You've got to take me down!'

'For heaven's sake, Jane, what on earth's wrong now?'

'It's my head. It feels odd . . .' She leaned on him more heavily still. 'Take me down, Colin.'

She felt rather than saw him turn to the man who had hesitated a few steps away.

'All right,' he said softly, 'I'll take you to the Bristol Hotel. You can rest there. The Bristol Hotel,' he repeated in a loud voice as he led her past the man down the slope.

All the way back in the taxi she was aware of Colin fidgeting by her side, trying to mask his anger.

'I'll have to stop at a chemist's,' she said weakly. 'I haven't any pills with me.'

'Really my dear, you shouldn't have come if you felt ill.'

'But I felt perfectly all right this morning,' she protested, and wished she could cry to order. Instead she fumbled for her handkerchief and pressed it against her face, keeping it there until Colin asked the taxi driver to stop outside a chemist.

'What sort of pills do you want?'

'See what they can recommend for migraine. Not too strong,' she said quickly.

With an incoherent mutter he got out of the taxi and hurried into the shop.

The moment he was out of sight Jane took a pencil and pad from her handbag and scribbled a name and phone number on it.

'I'd like you to telephone this message for me,' she said to the driver.

He grinned and shook his head and fear grew within her.

'Don't you speak English?'

He looked at her uncomprehendingly and she thrust the paper in front of his face. 'Telephone Mr. Aristophanes at this number and tell him the Bristol Hotel.'

The driver broke into a flood of Greek and taking the paper waved it in the direction of the shop.

'No, no, don't take it in there!' Jane saw Colin coming out of the chemist's and she turned back to the driver and pressed her finger to her lips, rolling her eyes heavenward in a gesture of fear. The man looked at her with instant comprehension and broke into another spate of Greek, stuffing the paper in his breast pocket as he did so.

'I managed to get some pills for you,' Colin said, stepping into the taxi. 'You have to take them and drink something hot. They'll work about twenty minutes later.'

'It's very kind of you,' Jane murmured, and half fell against him as the taxi turned sharply round the corner and drew to a stop outside the flight of steps leading to the Bristol.

They stepped out, and as Colin paid the driver Jane looked at the man and pointed to his breast pocket. He stared back at her unwinkingly, but as Colin turned away he gave her a wide smile and pointed to the commissionaire, standing on the pavement. Hope revived in her and as they moved towards the hotel she stopped by the commissionaire and spoke to him.

'Lovely day, isn't it?'

'It sure is,' he replied, a heavy American accent overlaying his English.

She smiled at him and hurried after Colin. So he did

speak English and she had not misjudged the taxi driver's intention.

Knowing she would still have to play for time, for even when Mr. Aristophanes got the message it would take him a while to arrive at the hotel, she set about being as difficult as she could. She refused to take the pills with coffee and insisted on having tea. But when it came it was too weak and had to be sent back again.

'Are you sure you wouldn't like to lie down?' Colin suggested. 'I'll have a word with the manager and see if he can arrange a room for you.'

'Will you come and sit with me? I don't want to be left alone.'

Colin shook his head and glanced at the entrance. 'I'll wait here. The manager mightn't like it if I stayed in the room with you.'

'Then I won't go!'

A waiter came over to their table with a fresh pot of tea, and knowing she could not hedge any more, Jane allowed Colin to pour her a cup and hand her two tablets. She swallowed them fearfully, hoping they would not make her ill, and then sipped her tea. The waiter was standing in her line of vision, but as he moved she saw a pale crumpled suit in the doorway. Excitement shivered through her. She had been right after all! The man walked in the direction of their table, veering to the left as he neared them, as though intending to sit at the next table. He was almost abreast of them when he hesitated and then stopped. 'Forgive me,' he said in sibilant English. 'But did I not see you a short while ago at the Acropolis?'

'Why, yes,' Colin said. 'But I don't remember—'

'I was admiring the temple when I noticed your wife take ill.'

Colin smiled. 'Not my wife – a friend of mine. She has a very bad headache.'

'That is indeed a shame. Is there anything I can do?'

'No, thank you,' Jane said quickly, 'but perhaps you'd like

to join us for a cup of tea?'

'Thank you.' The man sat down at once.

'What a coincidence your following us to hotel,' Jane said.

'I did not follow you.' The man turned in his chair to look at her and she saw the sweaty shine on his face and the open pores on his nose. 'But it was a happy coincidence, if I may say so, since it has given me an opportunity to air my English.'

He moved his chair a little closer to Colin and she wondered whether Colin would try to pass the diamond to him or whether they were going to arrange yet another meeting. But the more they were seen together the more dangerous it was and she was certain the jewel would change hands now. Once the man had it he would disappear, and if he did so before Mr. Aristophanes had the message . . . She had to do something to create a delay – anything, no matter what it was.

With a sweeping gesture and a murmur of 'Oh, my head,' she slumped forward across the table, sending the contents of her teacup over Colin's suit.

'Watch out!' He jumped up, but it was too late. A large stain was spreading over his jacket.

'I'm sorry,' she gasped. 'But I had such a pain . . . I couldn't see.' She stood up and with her handkerchief tried to rub away the mark.

'Don't, Jane, you're making it worse.' He stared down at himself. 'What a sight I look!'

'I'm afraid you'll have to go back to the boat and change.'

'I can't go back to the boat. My things are already packed.'

'Packed? Why, are you leaving the ship?'

'Yes.' He sat down again and motioned her to do the same. 'I only decided on the spur of the moment – last night, in fact.'

'I wish you'd told me.' She tried to look pathetic. 'I'll hate staying on board without you.'

'You needn't worry about Stephen. I heard he's leaving the ship too.'

'I still don't see why you've kept it such a secret,' she murmured.

'It isn't a secret.' Colin's control was beginning to fray. 'I was going to tell you at the Acropolis, but you were taken ill.'

'I see.' She was aware of the other man looking at his watch and knew he was impatient to leave.

'Where's your luggage, then?' she asked. 'If you'd like to go and change I can stay here and wait for you.'

'I haven't checked in at a hotel yet. It's at – it's at the station.'

He stopped speaking as the waiter came over and re-moved the tea-tray, watching with ill-concealed impatience as he wiped the table.

'I honestly think it would be best for you to go to a room and lie down until your headache's gone. If you don't like being by yourself I'll – I'll follow you up in a few minutes.'

She could not think of any other way to delay things and slowly stood up.

'Won't you come with me, Colin? I won't know where to go.'

The fullness left his mouth, and it became a thin, hard line.

'For goodness' sake stop acting like a baby. You're not the Belton heiress now! Have a word with the manager and I'll come and see you a little later.'

With dragging steps she walked across the carpeted lounge, and as she reached the door saw four men enter the lobby; three of them were tall and heavily built, un-mistakably bearing the stamp of plain-clothes detectives; the fourth was small and grey-haired, and Jane ran towards him.

'Mr. Aristophanes?'

'At your service. Miss Berry?'

She nodded and glanced quickly behind her. 'They're having tea together. I tried to delay things. I was afraid they were going to part.'

Mr. Aristophanes nodded to the henchmen behind him. 'Wait here a moment, Miss Berry. This won't take long.'

Light-footed, hardly seeming to touch the carpet, he ran to the lounge, and Jane, her overwhelming feeling one of relief, walked to the far corner of the lobby and sat down in a high-backed chair. From the lounge came the sound of a crashing table, a yell of anger and a shot.

The three policemen came from the lounge, two of them holding the man in the crumpled suit, who was shouting at them in Greek, the third handcuffed to Colin. He looked as imperturbable as ever, his face pale and pink, his mouth slightly smiling. Jane crouched back in her chair, willing herself not to be seen. But she had reckoned without Mr. Aristophanes, for he looked in her direction and called her name. Colin stopped walking, and Jane, wishing she were a million miles away, came slowly towards him.

The silver-blond head turned inquiringly from the Greek to Jane and back again.

'You two know one another?'

'Miss Berry's father is well acquainted with me,' the man said.

Colin looked at Jane. 'So you were more than just a reporter posing as an heiress?'

'Yes.'

'When did you find out about me?'

'When you dropped the gold coin in my cabin.'

'How careless of me.' His eyelids drooped over his eyes and then slowly lifted. 'When you write up the story, Jane, try not to make it too lurid. I mean, I'm not the only man to have been fooled by a pretty blonde, am I?'

She half smiled. 'Don't worry, Colin. This is one story I don't intend writing.'

'Thanks, my dear. I appreciate that.'

163

Mr. Aristophanes interrupted them. 'Will you be coming to the station with us, Miss Berry?'

'Not unless I have to. I'd really like to return to England today.'

'I will see if I can arrange it. I'll leave a message with Reception and if I can get you a seat I'll send a car to take you to the airport.'

At midday Jane returned to the hotel and the reception clerk told her that Mr. Aristophanes had managed to procure a seat for her on the afternoon plane to London. For the next few hours she wandered round Athens, aware of the city yet not really appreciating it; pausing only to look at the long line of flower shops opposite the main square, where she smelled the heady fragrance of roses and carnations. She was glad when it was time to leave for the airport and a large limousine came to collect her. Her surprise was great to find Mr. Aristophanes in the back seat, a box of chocolates in his hand which he presented to her as she took her place beside him.

'You were a very brave girl,' he said. 'I'm sure the insurance company will reward you.'

'I wouldn't want anything. It was a horrible feeling, Mr. Aristophanes. I knew Colin quite well and—'

'Ah yes. It is always bad when one knows them. Myself I have had experience of it many times. Still, it will be a great relief to your father to have Waterman in custody.'

'What will happen to him?'

'He will be sent back to London for trial.'

Jane looked at the houses flashing past and sighed.

'It was the gold coin that gave him away,' she said. 'It seemed so pointless to carry it around.'

'It was their means of identification. Waterman did not work alone, as you know, and there are many other men we have yet to find. It is not only jewellery that they steal, but also paintings, and we are pretty sure they organized the recent Paris theft. It is for the disposing of these sort of things that an organization is needed. Jewellery is not so difficult to get rid of. Waterman worked on his own when he took the Lorenz Diamond and the cross, but I am certain he worked with other men too. And these are the ones we must still search for.'

'You'll have to count me out.' Jane shivered. 'I'm never going to do anything like this again.'

Mr. Aristophanes patted her hand. 'Have a chocolate,' he said. 'They are very sweet and will take away the taste of bitterness.'

CHAPTER TWELVE

RAIN was glistening on the tarmac as Jane arrived at Heathrow, and as she came out of the Customs and into the terminal, her father rose from an armchair and enveloped her in an unusually demonstrative hug.

Driving home, she told him everything that had happened, only leaving out the one fact she could not bear to remember – her love for Stephen Drake. Her father had already spoken to Mr. Aristophanes on the telephone, but he was eager to have a first-hand account of everything, and by the time she had finished they had drawn up outside their house.

'I was glad Mr. Aristophanes didn't ask me to bring the diamond back,' she said, walking up to the front door.

'Old Arry isn't as casual as he appears,' Tom Berry laughed, and stepped aside for Jane to enter the hall.

She did so and gave a sigh of pleasure. The carpet might be threadbare, the walls in need of a coat of paint, but it was home, the place where she belonged. Never again would she try to enter an alien world or be foolish enough to believe that love could bridge any gulf.

'A nice cup of English tea,' her father said, and propelled her into the kitchen. 'Sit down, and I'll make it for you.'

He was as good as his word, and within a few moments they were sitting either side of the table drinking strong tea and munching biscuits.

'Not like the *Cambrian*, eh?' he grinned. 'I hear there's a waiter for every passenger.'

'They're welcome to it. It's not the sort of life for me.'

'No millionaires in tow? I was anticipating you'd come back with a diamond of your own!'

'Millionaires don't become engaged so quickly,' she said lightly. 'Anyway, money marries money.'

'Not according to the *Morning Star*! They're always discovering Cinderella stories. If I remember rightly, you discovered a few of them yourself.'

'Well, I won't be doing *that* any more. I've resigned.'

'Why?'

'Stephen Drake – I told you he was on board – objected to my not telling him of my identity. We had a row and – and gave in my notice.'

She could tell from his expression that her father knew there was more to the story than she told him, and she was glad that he did not question her.

'Anyway,' she went on, 'I'm tired of reporting. I want to find a job where I needn't snoop into people's lives and make up lies when truth isn't stranger than fiction!'

'Why not forget about work for the time being? The Metropolitan are delighted with the job I did – or rather the job you did for me – and they've renewed my contract and upped my salary. The least I can do is to give you the benefit of it, and I don't see why you can't take a long holiday. Even go on the next *Cambrian* cruise as yourself!'

'Never. I don't want to see any of those people again.' She poured herself another cup of tea. 'What will happen to Colin? Will he be held responsible for Hawton's death?'

'I'm afraid we won't be holding him responsible for anything,' Tom Berry said slowly. 'He's facing someone more fitted than any of us to decide on responsibility.'

There was no mistaking the portentousness of the words, and Jane put down her cup.

'What's happened to him?'

'I didn't tell you before because I knew you'd be upset . . . But Arry told me on the telephone – the reason he rang, in fact – that they were taking Waterman to the airport to put him on the plane after yours when he opened the car door and jumped out. Another car was overtaking them at the time and—' he spread out his hands – 'it was all over in seconds.'

Jane's eyes filled with tears and she did not bother to wipe them away. 'I'm glad he didn't have to stand trial. It would have been horrible. I know I shouldn't feel sympathy for him, but—'

'You didn't feel sympathy, my dear – you felt pity, and I can't blame you for that.' Her father reached for his pipe and put it between his lips. 'Go to bed, Jane. Have a good night's sleep and put the whole thing from your mind.'

Jane stood up. 'Claire will be pleased it's ended this way. A trial might have given her some unwelcome publicity – especially if she'd been called as a witness.'

'She certainly *would* have been, and damned lucky not to be charged as an accessory too. Still, women of that type always have things made easy for them. Luck, I suppose you'd call it.'

Jane decided not to see Frank Preston immediately. He did not know of her return and she was anxious to wait until the excitement of Colin Waterman's death had died down. But the main reason – one which she did not even want to admit to herself – was that she was waiting to hear from Stephen, and every time the telephone rang, every time there was a knock at the door, her heart leapt in her throat.

But the week drew to a close without any word from him and she was forced to accept the fact that he did not intend to get in touch with her.

'I didn't expect him to tell me he still loved me,' she admitted to herself on the Sunday night, when she had finally give up all hope of hearing from him. 'I just hoped he'd have the decency to apologize for the things he'd said, for the way he behaved when I came out of Colin's cabin.' She buried her head in her hands: would she ever forget the humiliation of his kisses, the callous touch of his hands . . .?

First thing on Monday morning she went to see Frank Preston, and her belief that he would try and persuade her not to resign was shattered almost by his first words.

'What a rocket I got from Drake. If I'd any idea he was

going to be on board, I'd never have asked you to go.'

'I didn't go because you asked me,' she said firmly, determined to clear up this point once and for all. 'I went because of my father. It had nothing to do with your threatening to fire me.'

'I realized that as soon as the news of Waterman broke. You were a pretty brave girl.'

'Thank you.' She half smiled. 'I'm glad you didn't ask me to tell you the "story in my own words".'

He gave a surly grunt. 'Don't remind me of the scoop we missed. I can tell you right now I was planning on running it – full page spread and—'

'I wouldn't have written it,' she interrupted quickly.

'You would by the time *I'd* finished with you!' He swivelled in his chair. 'But Drake was so precise in what he said about you that I didn't have the nerve to use your name in the paper.'

She moistened her lips. 'What do you – what do you mean?'

Preston leaned forward. 'I don't know what happened between the two of you, and I'm not asking. But he made it pretty plain that you're never to do anything for the *Star* again. That's why I wasn't surprised when you told me you weren't going to come back here.'

'I see. When did Stephen – when did Mr. Drake tell you this?'

'We got a cable from him when he was in Athens.'

The shock of hearing this was so great that Jane could not move. All the questions that had seethed in her mind for the past week were now answered, completing the final and ultimate humiliation of knowing that Stephen thought so little of her that he did not care even to pretend to the courtesy of an apology.

'I'm sorry things had to end this way,' Frank Preston broke into her thoughts. 'I've been told to give you a cheque for six months' salary and—'

'I don't want it.' She stood up and without another word

169

walked out.

The same day she applied for and was offered the job of copywriter at Foster's Advertising Agency, using her friendship with one of the publicists there to obtain an interview with Robert Foster himself, a dynamic Anglo-American in his late thirties. She liked him on sight and instinctively felt that he liked her. Indeed, she was almost certain his liking prompted him to give her the job, for the copy test she did was no better than average.

A week after she had joined the Agency, Robert Foster called her into his office and asked her to dine with him. Reluctant though she was to antagonize him, the thought of making conversation with another man, and pretending to a gaiety she did not feel, was more than she could bear, and even though she knew it might lose her the job, she had to refuse him.

But in this she had done him an injustice, for he accepted her rebuff with a smile and there was no outward change in his demeanour. If anything he became friendlier, including her in some of the interviews he had with less important clients.

'You've a good brain and you're a quick thinker,' he said on one occasion. 'All you lack is experience in this work, but I'm pretty sure in a few months you'll be way ahead of any of the other copywriters here.'

'I wish I could get excited about that,' she admitted truthfully. 'But after reporting, this seems so dull. I mean, there's a limit to what one can say about boot polish or shaving cream!'

'Don't you believe it,' he said dryly. 'Genius comes in your ability to ring the changes, to say the same thing in a different way. Besides, I've other plans for you – but I'm prepared to wait a while on those!'

There had also been no word from Janey Belton, and reluctant to presume on their acquaintance – since Janey's silence implied that she wanted to forget it – Jane only penned her a short note when she returned the key of the jewel-case, saying that she hoped Dinky Howard had by now sent it back to her, together with all the clothes which she had left packed in the stateroom. There was no reply from Janey, merely a typewritten acknowledgment from Cedric Belton's secretary saying that the letter and its enclosure had been received.

She was therefore surprised when, returning home the following Friday, she found a Rolls parked outside the house and Janey Belton standing beside it.

'I'd almost given you up,' the girl cried. 'I've been here hours!'

'If you'd let me know you were coming—'

'I couldn't. I got back from the States this morning and came straight over. Dad's secretary told me you'd returned the key of my jewel-case and gave me your letter.'

'She should have told me you were away,' Jane said as she opened the front door and led the way into the sitting-room. 'When you didn't reply yourself I assumed you didn't want to see me again.'

'Why ever not?' Janey's head tilted imperiously, the blonde hair glinting in the light. 'I meant to write to you when I was in New York, but I'd forgotten your address and Dad wouldn't let me write to you c/o your Features Editor in case he opened it. You know what newspapermen are like.'

Jane shook her head. Frank Preston's integrity was negligible if he felt there was a good story to be had, but she doubted whether even he would resort to opening letters not addressed to him.

'It doesn't matter,' she said. 'The main thing is that you're here. But tell me, did my taking your place help you at all? When I was in Venice I learned that your father had found out the truth.'

Janey made a face. 'I'm surprised you didn't *hear* him as well! Lord, the way he shouted! Still, it's all over now – and I've won.'

'Won?'

'Yes.' Janey held out her hand on which shone an engagement ring, the diamonds so small as to be almost indiscernible. 'Dad's agreed to my marrying Ted,' she giggled. 'I told him that though the cruise idea hadn't worked, I had lots more ideas up my sleeve. I think I frightened him to death – he began to imagine the sort of escapades I'd get up to – so he had a long talk with Ted and finally said yes. Oh, Jane, I'm so happy I think I'm going to burst. And it's all because of you. If you hadn't gone on the cruise instead of me, none of this would have happened.'

'I'm glad something's turned out right.'

Egoist though she was, Janey sensed the irony in the words. 'Didn't *you* enjoy yourself? I thought you'd have had a wonderful time.'

'I did.'

'You're lying. I can tell from your voice.' Janey was not her father's daughter for nothing. 'Come on, tell me the truth. What went wrong?'

'Nothing. I tell you I had a wonderful time.'

'Even when you nabbed Colin Waterman?'

Jane looked up sharply. 'How do you know about that? The papers only mentioned that an English girl had helped in his capture. They didn't give my name.'

'I met a girl in the States called Claire Saunders. She assumed you'd told me the whole story. I got the impression she'd had a pretty sticky interview with Scotland Yard herself.' Janey twisted the ring on her hand and looked at it admiringly. 'I can't say I liked her much, though I sympathized with her for not giving the man away. After all, they'd known each other since they were children. Anyway, let's forget her. I've more important things to talk about. My wedding for one; and your being a bridesmaid for another.'

'A bridesmaid?'

'Yes. Dad's paying for the clothes, so you've no excuse for refusing.'

'I wouldn't dream of refusing. I'd love to be your bridesmaid.'

'Good.' Janey glanced at her watch. 'I must dash now. If there's one thing Ted can't stand it's being kept waiting.' At the door she paused and put her arm round Jane's shoulder. 'I'd love you to meet him soon. Are you free to have dinner with us tomorrow night?'

'I'd love to.'

'Good. Let's make it the Savoy. The Grill Room at eight. And bring a man if you want to.'

In a flurry of skirts she ran down the path, and Jane returned to the sitting-room. Janey's happiness served to remind her of the difference in their lives, made her realize that though she still loved Stephen she could not allow him to ruin her future. It was stupid to go on refusing the dates that had come her way since she had changed jobs, or to keep rebuffing Robert Foster, for though he had not repeated his offer of dinner, she knew she had only to give the slightest hint of a change of attitude for him to start bombarding her with invitations.

'I'm not going to mope any more,' she said out loud. 'Enough's enough!'

True to her word, she took the first opportunity to go into his office the next day, using some ad. copy as her excuse. After he had seen it she did not immediately leave, a sufficient change in behaviour for him to notice.

'How come you're not rushing out on me?' he asked. 'Aren't you scared of me any longer?'

'I was never scared,' she laughed, 'merely careful!'

'And does your sitting here mean that you're no longer being careful?'

She grinned, and he grinned back at her.

'Miss Berry, ma'am, will you do me the honour of having dinner with me tonight?'

'Yes, please,' she said. 'But can *you* come as my guest? I've been invited to the Savoy.'

He came round the side of the desk and stood next to her, only a little taller than she was, yet with the assured grace of

173

an athlete. 'I know there's a great big mystery tied up in your past, Jane, and I'm not going to pry into your affairs. I just want you to know that I'm glad you're starting to think in terms of the future again, and I hope you'll include me. I'm a patient guy, and I'd like you to look on me as a friend, a sort of sheep in wolf's clothes!'

'A very nice sheep,' she said. 'Thanks, Bob, I will.'

Dinner at the Savoy turned out to be much nicer than Jane had anticipated. With Ted, Janey was a different person; hanging on to his every word, agreeing with what he said and leaving him to do most of the talking.

'You're not a bit the way I imagine,' Ted said to Jane during a temporary lull in the conversation. 'Whenever one thinks of reporters one—'

'I know,' she interrupted. 'But honestly, I'm just an ordinary girl.'

'Not ordinary. There aren't many girls who'd have the nerve to impersonate my beloved fiancée!'

They all laughed, Janey most of all. 'I don't see why you should give Jane credit for being brave,' she said. 'Why, she rang up the night before and told me she'd changed her mind.'

Ted raised his eyebrows. 'So you *did* get cold feet?'

'Yes.' Alcohol had loosened Jane's tongue and she felt no embarrassment in admitting her reasons. 'I didn't want to snoop on innocent people. I wanted to help Janey and I'd have agreed to the impersonation if I needn't have written the articles. But I couldn't see Frank Preston allowing me to go on the cruise in those circumstances!'

'What made you change your mind all over again?'

Briefly she spoke of her father's job with the Metropolitan Insurance Company, of her realization that only she could help him. But though she glossed over the story, Janey's eyes gleamed with excitement.

'How absolutely thrilling! So it's really your father I've got to thank for your going on the cruise. He'll have to be bridesmaid at my wedding too!' She giggled. 'The least we can do is to drink a toast to him.' She raised her arms to attract the attention of their waiter and then stopped, her expression changing. 'Well, well, look who's just come in.'

Jane turned, her body tensing as she saw Claire, lovelier than ever in a simple black dress, diamonds sparkling at her throat and wrists. But it was not the girl who caused her to lose colour, but the man walking directly behind her. Stephen.

Seen in casual clothes on the sun deck he had looked handsome, but here, in this glamorous setting among beautifully gowned women and well-groomed expense-account men, he stood out head and shoulders. 'And not just physically, either,' she thought, for he exuded a dynamism that made all heads turn to watch him.

'Can anyone tell me the name of that gorgeous hunk of man?' Janey asked.

'Stephen Drake,' Jane said quickly. 'He was on the – he was on the *Cambrian*.'

'What a pity I didn't know,' Janey giggled. 'Who is he?'

'He owns the paper Jane used to work for,' Bob Foster replied. 'A tycoon with a capital T.'

Janey's reply was forestalled by Claire and Stephen walking past their table. 'Hello, Claire,' she called.

Claire stopped, her smile artificial. 'Hello, Janey!' She put her hand on Stephen's arm. 'Darling, would you like to meet the *real* Janey Belton?'

Stephen nodded, murmured a polite greeting and looked so obviously anxious to move on that Claire gave them an apologetic glance and followed him.

'Well, well,' Janey said. 'I *did* get the frozen mitt!'

Bob looked at Jane. 'So did you. Didn't he remember who you were?'

'Too well.' Aware of the curious eyes of the three people around her, she felt some explanation was necessary. 'He was furious when he found out I was one of his reporters.'

'Why?' Janey asked indignantly. 'Couldn't he take a joke?'

'Not when he thought it was on him.'

'What do you mean?'

'Nothing,' Jane said. 'I was talking for the sake of talking.'

Janey appeared to be satisfied with this reply, but when they were in the cloakroom collecting their coats she broached the subject again.

'You don't normally talk just for the sake of talking. What really gives between you and that dreamboat? I mean, it took no imagination to see he was absolutely livid with you.'

'We quarrelled.'

'That much I gathered! You looked like a ghost when you saw him. If I didn't know you better I'd have said you were in love with him.'

Jane turned away, but not quickly enough to hide the tears in her eyes.

'Gosh, Jane. Then it's true! I'm awfully sorry. I'd never have teased you if I'd known.'

'Why should you know? It's just one of those things.'

'I don't believe he's indifferent to you. If he was he wouldn't have ignored you just now. What happened?'

Jane sighed. 'When he found out what I was he assumed I'd gone on the cruise to find a rich husband as well as a story.'

'Why should he think that?'

'Because I didn't tell him my identity at the very beginning.'

'Why didn't you?'

'I'd promised my father,' Jane said wearily.

'I see. Well, you'd have thought he'd have realized by now why you couldn't tell him.'

Jane nodded miserably. 'His own paper featured Colin's arrest on the front page.'

Janey put on her mink jacket, her expression thoughtful. 'We'd better go. Bob and Ted will be wondering what's happened to us.'

They walked out of the cloakroom and up the stairs. 'Why don't you go and see Stephen? Maybe he's waiting for you to—'

'I'll never go and see him. Never!'

'What about *my* going?'

'Don't you dare!' Jane seized the other girl's arm. 'You must promise me you won't go.'

'Come on, girls,' Ted called. 'The taxi's waiting.'

It was only later as she was lying in bed that Jane remembered that Janey had not given her the promise she had asked for. 'I'll ring her in the morning,' she thought sleepily. 'The last thing I want is for Stephen to think I'm running after him.'

But in the morning, when she telephoned the Belton house, she was told that Janey had gone to Paris for a few days to choose her trousseau, and by the end of the week her desire to extract the promise had abated: after all, Janey would be far too busy with her own affairs to bother with anyone else's.

It was not until some ten days later that the two girls met at the beige and gilt salon of the fashion house, where the bridesmaids' dresses were being made. Janey looked lovelier than ever, her sparkle and vitality a striking contrast to Jane's pallor and fragility.

'I wish you'd been able to come to Paris with me,' she said. 'Dad didn't let me out of his sight for a minute!'

'Wasn't Ted with you?'

'He only came over for the week-end.' Janey tilted her head. 'From the look of you, it would have done you good to have come with him. You look ghastly.'

Aware of the shadows beneath her eyes and the hollows that had appeared on her cheekbones, Jane essayed a laugh. 'I've been living it up too much.'

'Every time Madame comes to try on her dress,' the fitter said reproachfully, 'we have to take in the waist.'

'All to the good. Paris has decreed waists are back again!'

'So are bosoms,' Janey intervened. 'And if you lose any more weight, you won't have one!'

Jane pretended not to hear, concentrating instead on the hemline and whether or not it should be shorter. The decision settled, the fitter helped her out of the dress and took it away, leaving her to put on her own clothes.

'Are you still seeing Bob Foster?' Janey asked.

'Yes, quite a bit.'

'I'm glad. Any romance in the offing?'

'No.' Jane's voice was muffled beneath her dress as she slipped it over her head. 'And not likely to be either. I don't love him.'

'I suppose it's still Stephen Drake?'

There was no need for any reply; the sudden flush to the curve of Jane's cheek was answer enough.

Janey stood up. 'I've masses to do. Do you mind awfully if I don't wait for you?'

'Of course not.'

With a quick hug, the younger girl hurried from the cubicle and Jane slowly finished dressing and followed her.

'What a beautiful bride Miss Belton will make,' one of the vendeuses said. 'I always think blondes look particularly lovely in white.' She glanced at Jane's corn-coloured hair. 'Are *you* engaged, Madame?'

'No, I'm not.'

'Well, I do hope we'll have the pleasure of dressing you when the happy day comes.'

The smile stiff on her face, Jane stepped into the street. Her day would never come unless she were able to put Stephen out of her mind. A change of job had done little to help and she wondered whether a change of country might not be the next move.

She mentioned this to her father later that evening, and he received the news without surprise.

'I've been expecting you to say this since you got back from Greece. I knew there was something in the wind when you left the paper.' He puffed at his pipe. 'Running away won't help, you know. If you're upset about anything, you'd be better off to face it.'

'There's nothing to face.' Although she had never before discussed her emotional life with her father, she knew that now was not the time for pretence. 'I'm in love with a man who doesn't love me and that's all there is to it. I hoped that changing my job would help me to forget him, but I was wrong.'

'A change of country won't do the trick either. What you need is a change of man! Foster seems very fond of you. Why not give him a chance?'

'Because it isn't fair to him.' She sighed. 'He's asked me to marry him and I've refused.'

Her father grunted. 'You're not cut out to be an old maid. You might not think you'll fall in love again, but I'm willing to bet you will. The only question is how miserable you're going to make your life in the interim.'

Jane asked herself the same question as she went up to her room that night. How long would it be before the memory of Stephen dimmed? At the moment she had only to clear her eyes to see his face, to feel the touch of his lips and the pressure of his body. With an exclamation she walked over to the window and breathed in the cool air. In the distance a clock chimed twelve, and she sighed. Where was he now? Dancing with Claire or another woman? Or was he perhaps in Fleet Street looking at the early editions of his paper? Wherever he was and whatever he was doing she was sure of one thing: he was giving no thought to the girl who had once worked for him, whom he had admitted he might have loved had the circumstances been different.

'But he didn't trust me,' she said aloud, 'and without trust there can be no love.'

CHAPTER THIRTEEN

In the weeks that followed Jane forced herself to accept her father's advice and, as if sensing her change of attitude, Bob Foster insisted on seeing her as often as possible. Gradually she began to rely on him more, to think of him as a part of her life, though there were still occasions when her heart beat fast at the sight of a tanned face or a dark head glimpsed in a crowd.

At last the great day drew near and Jane travelled down to the magnificent Queen Anne house where the Beltons lived. It was set in acres of woodland and was exactly the sort of background she had assumed her friend would have, 'The sort of background that all the women in Stephen's life would have too,' she thought bitterly as she entered the room that had been given to her and looked round at the opulent furnishings.

As soon as she had unpacked she went along to her friend's bedroom and knocked on the door.

'Come in,' came the gay answer. 'If you can manage to find enough space!'

Jane stepped inside, laughing as she saw the confusion. The entire room seemed to be swamped with clothes: evening dresses and afternoon dresses were strewn side by side and the bed was heaped with piles of pastel-coloured lingerie, the floor covered with shoes and slippers and sandals. In the midst of it all stood the future bride, her blonde hair shining in the sunlight, her eyes sparkling and full of happiness.

'You don't intend taking all these clothes away with you?' Jane asked in mock horror.

'Every single one.'

'But you'll never wear them.'

'Of course I will. We're going for a month, you know. It's

Dad's wedding present to us. Just think of it – four lovely weeks in the Bahamas. Even Ted's excited, though he tries to pretend he isn't.'

'Any chance of my taking your place on this trip?'

'Not likely! Anyway, you'll be having your own honeymoon before long.'

'I doubt it.'

'We'll see.' There was a strange look on Janey's face. 'My intuition tells me you'll be a Mrs. before the year's out.'

'If Bob's asked you to—'

'Bob hasn't said a word.' Janey rummaged in her jewelcase and extracted the ruby necklace. 'I'd like you to wear this tomorrow. It'll go with your dress.'

'I'd rather not, thanks. It reminds me of Colin.'

Janey was taken by surprise. 'Do you mean you still think about him?'

'Yes. It's horrible to be responsible for another person's death.'

'What rot! You were only doing your duty. Honestly, you're crazy to give him another thought. He was a thief and a murderer too, from what you've told me. Anyway, take a leaf out of Claire's book. *She* doesn't appear to have lost any sleep over him.'

Jane walked over to the window and looked out at the beautifully kept lawns. 'Have you seen her lately?' she asked, her voice casual.

'I haven't seen her with Stephen Drake, if that's what you mean.' Janey's voice was half hidden in the wardrobe and when she spoke again it was to comment on her wedding dress. 'I hope Ted's going to like it. I wanted a slinky skirt myself, but I knew he fancied something pretty-pretty! Gosh, only tonight to get though and then I'll be his wife.'

They intended to go to bed early that night, but Janey's spirits were too volatile to let her rest, and though Ted did not appear, half a dozen other young people arrived, mostly school friends of Janey's. Watching them together, Jane was once again conscious of coming from a different world, of being older than her years.

Knowing she would not be missed, she went to bed, but sleep would not come and she watched the sky turn from black to grey and then rosy pink, falling into slumber as the first early birds began their chorus.

It was ten-thirty before she awakened, and only then because an anxious maid came in with her breakfast tray, warning her that she had barely an hour before she was due to leave for the church. She washed in the luxurious peach-mirrored bathroom that reminded her of the *Cambrian* and slipped into the shell pink brassière and pantees that matched her dress. Carefully she applied her make-up, though nothing could completely hide the lavender shadows under her eyes nor disguise the thinness of her face. Yet she knew she had never looked lovelier, for tiredness and pallor gave her an ethereal aura heightened by the deceptively simple dress, with its round-necked bodice and graceful swirling skirt, the chiffon floating round her like morning mist.

Janey had left instructions that no one was to visit her other than the vendeuse who had come down to make sure the wedding dress was in order, and promptly at eleven she descended the stairs to the hall where her father, Jane and three child bridesmaids were waiting. It was the only occasion since she had known him that Jane could remember Cedric Belton losing his voice, and he stared in silence as his daughter glided towards him, a vision of loveliness in white tulle, her blonde hair held in place by a diamond tiara, her face softened by clouds of veiling.

'My little girl,' he said at last, his staccato voice broken. 'If that young man of yours doesn't make you happy, I'll – I'll tar and feather him!'

Janey giggled, and instantly the vision was brought down to earth. Giving Jane a wink, she waited with her father as the bridesmaids left for the church in their Rolls.

It was not until she entered the church and heard the organ pealing out the solemn strains of the bridal march that she was able to relax; for the first time in many weeks experiencing a feeling of peace. It was as if her unhappiness became insignificant in this atmosphere of reverence. The indefinable odour of a church compounded of waxed wood, flowers and freshly polished brass filled her nostrils and she breathed deeply, the trembling flowers in her hands becoming still.

Slowly the ceremony went on, the minister's voice booming in sepulchral tones as he led the young couple to the altar. Jane stepped forward to take the bride's bouquet, cradling it carefully until it was time to enter the vestry. Here in the small crowded room the legalities of the ceremony were completed, and then, in a flurry of hugs and kisses and the triumphant notes of Mendelssohn's march, they walked down the aisle.

Now Jane was able to see everyone clearly, as the bride made her slow, triumphal progress down the nave. In the shadow of one of the pillars she saw Bob, his usually smiling face strained and embarrassed. The corners of her mouth quirked with amusement. Like most men he found weddings a strain!

There was still a slight smile on her mouth as she took the last few steps and she was almost at the door before she noticed the man standing at the back of the church, holding himself aloof from the crowds. Their eyes met, hers dilated with fear, his narrow, probing. She trembled so violently that she was unable to walk, and the three little bridesmaids bumped against her. It was only their proximity that urged her into motion again, and keeping her head averted she walked out.

What was Stephen Drake doing here? Had Janey invited him in the hope that it might heal the breach between them? If so it had been ridiculous thing to do. And what must Bob think? Though he had never questioned her about Stephen she knew he was aware of her feelings for the man.

As she drove back to the Beltons' house anger overcame dismay, giving her the necessary impetus to get through the next hour. The wedding breakfast seemed never-ending, and though she was unable to eat any of the sumptuous food, she drank two glasses of champagne. The sharp and painful outlines of reality became blurred, softening her attitude to Bob, making it easy for her to smile at him, to let him hold her hand.

'You look so beautiful,' he murmured. 'I wish you'd let me take care of you.'

'You're doing very well,' she said, tilting her glass at him. 'I don't want anything more, thanks.'

'I wasn't thinking about food and drink!'

'Please, Bob, don't.' She sipped her champagne, wrinkling her nose at the bubbles. 'I don't want to talk seriously about anything at the moment. This is Janey's wedding, remember? Let's just think about her.'

'Why not just think about weddings?'

She shook her head, and with a sigh he picked up his own glass. 'Did you see Stephen Drake in church?' he asked.

She nodded. 'I was surprised Janey invited him. Is Claire Saunders here too?'

'Not as far as I know. Though if he came with her it would explain the invitation.'

'If you want an explanation,' Jane said lightly. 'Stephen's coming over to us now.'

She watched him approach, only her sudden instinctive movement towards Bob indicating that she was not inwardly as calm as she outwardly appeared. How handsome he looked in his grey jacket and stiff white shirt, its very formality heightening his air of detachment. Not that there was anything very detached in his expression, for he seemed anxious, a flush on his cheekbones, his mouth not quite steady.

'Hello, Stephen,' she said lightly. 'Bob and I were just talking about you. I don't think you remember Bob, do you?'

She effected the introductions and the two men looked at one another warily.

'Bob Foster,' Stephen echoed the name. 'Are you connected with Foster's Agency?'

Bob nodded, and Stephen looked from him to Jane.

Intercepting the look, Bob put his hand on her arm. 'Jane works for me, though I'm trying to persuade her to do it in a less professional capacity!'

'Bob, don't,' Jane said quickly. 'I'm sure Stephen isn't interested in our affairs.'

'But I *am*,' Stephen intervened. 'Extremely interested. Would I be precipitate in offering my congratulations?'

Pride would not let Jane say no, but honesty would not let her say yes, and she prevaricated by raising her glass to her lips and allowing Bob to answer for her.

'A bit precipitate, I'm afraid. Jane's not an easy girl to persuade. But I'm hoping.'

'Aren't we all?' Stephen said, and with an abrupt movement turned away. Jane watched him disappear through the crowd, longing to run after him, to fling herself into his arms and beg him to tell her that he still loved her.

'But he never loved me,' she told herself fiercely. 'Never, never.'

The control she had kept upon herself was in danger of breaking, the champagne gaiety threatening to dissolve beneath the weight of her depression.

'Would you like to sit down?' Bob said in her ear, and without waiting for an answer pushed her into a chair that had just become vacant. 'What about another drink?'

She shook her head. 'I'll be all right in a minute. It's just the heat and the excitement.'

'And Stephen Drake.' His voice was low. 'Don't pretend with me, Jane. Stephen's the reason, isn't he?'

'The reason?'

'For turning me down. You fell in love with him on the cruise. I knew that when I saw the way he behaved at the Savoy. No man would have been so offhand with you unless he was fighting himself. What went wrong?'

'Nothing. Please, Bob, I don't want to talk about it. It was just the unexpectedness of seeing him that upset me. I'll be all right soon.'

She closed her eyes, but felt no relief. Her meeting with Stephen made her realize the futility of contemplating a future with Bob. As long as the sight of him could make her feel this way she had no chance of happiness with another man. The only solution was one she had been putting off for the last month: another country. Perhaps when they were oceans apart she would be able to make a new life for herself.

People milled around her, and conversation and laughter echoed loud in her ears. It became suddenly too much for her to bear and she stood up and thrust her glass into Bob's hands. 'Do you mind if I leave you for a bit? I must get away from this.'

'If you want a shoulder to lean on I'm still willing to oblige.'

'Leaning won't help. I've got to work this out alone.'

'Alone?' He caught her hand. 'You don't really mean alone, do you, Jane?'

'Yes, Bob, I do. I'm not the right girl for you, and it's wrong of me to pretend I ever can be.'

'You can,' he said softly. 'But will you?'

She shook her head and, touching his cheek with a shaking hand, slipped through the crowds and across the lawn. Lightfooted, she sped over the grass, through the formal rose gardens and down to the less cultivated part of the grounds. It was very beautiful here with flowers growing rough in the grass and a small brook bubbling over its bed of pebbles. A wooden seat stood beside a weeping willow and she sat down on it, her skirts falling around her in a pink cloud, her blonde hair falling forward to hide her face as she bent her head.

For a long while she sat beside the water, gaining peace from its incessant movement. A breeze began to play among the leaves, rustling them and lifting the edges of the chiffon around her feet. In the far distance she could hear the occasional hum of a car and knew that she would have to return to the house to say goodbye to Janey before she left on her honeymoon.

How disappointed her friend would be that her invitation to Stephen had not done what she had hoped. Jane stirred and reached for her handbag. She opened her compact and carefully smoothed powder underneath her eyes, making sure the tears had not blurred her mascara.

'I wouldn't worry about the way you look,' a deep voice said behind her. With automatic gestures she closed the compact and put it back into her handbag before raising her head and looking at Stephen, who was standing a few yards away.

'I didn't know you were here.'

'I've been looking for you,' he replied. 'I must have gone through every room in that damned house.'

'You were clever to find me.'

'I'd have found you, no matter where you were,' he said roughly. 'I've got to talk to you.'

'We've nothing to say to each other.'

'You mightn't have anything to say to *me*, but I've a lot to say to you!' He strode over and looked as though he wanted to pull her to her feet, but thought better of it.

'First of all I owe you an apology for misjudging you. If you hadn't hurt my pride I'd never have acted the way I did. It was a shock finding out you didn't have the courage to tell me who you were and—'

'It wasn't a question of courage,' she interrupted. 'I'd promised my father.'

'I realized that when Janey—'

'When Janey . . .? Do you mean she's been to see you?'

'Yes. She came a few days ago. I wanted to see you at once, but she made me promise to wait until today. She wanted to feel that we'd come together on her wedding day.' His voice died, but he came close and caught her hands. 'Will you forgive me, Jane?'

She tilted her head and looked into his face, loving him

more dearly at this moment than at any time before, yet knowing that no matter how she loved him they had no future together.

'Of course I'll forgive you, Stephen.'

'Thank God for that. Oh, my darling —'

'No, don't call me that.' She pulled her hands away from his and moved back. 'Because I forgive you it doesn't mean things can be the same between us.'

'But why not? You're not in love with Foster, are you?'

'I don't change my affections as quickly as that. And I don't think *you* can change so quickly either. You doubted me, Stephen, and that hurts me very much. You didn't believe in me until Janey had been to see you, but what did she say to make you change your mind? Did she tell you I was still pining for you? That I wasn't interested in your money? Did she —'

'Stop it,' he said sharply. 'Janey only came to tell me what a swine I was! In the course of the conversation she also happened to mention Colin and the Lorenz Diamond.' Stephen's voice was heavy with anguish. 'Don't you understand what I'm trying to tell you? I didn't know the truth until I'd spoken to her.'

'What did you have to know, Stephen?' she said contemptuously. 'Couldn't you trust your heart? I told you once before that you can't have a real relationship without trust and understanding. You knew why I was nice to Colin, why I was in his cabin that night, and yet you still didn't believe in me, you still had to wait for Janey to come and make you see reason. Well, if that's the sort of love you can offer I don't want it. I don't want it,' she reiterated.

'You've got it all wrong.' He strode over to her, his hands heavy on her shoulders, the vein in his forehead pulsing as it always did when he was moved. 'Do you think I was waiting for someone to make me see reason? Do you think I'm the sort of man who would never admit when he was wrong?'

'Look how long it's taken you. Months! That night in the Savoy you treated me as if I were a stranger.'

'I didn't know about Colin then! That night at the Savoy I still believed everything I'd said to you on the ship.'

She looked at him in amazement, and his eyes looked directly into hers.

'I left the ship the moment we docked at Athens,' he said, 'and went to stay on one of the islands with a friend of mine. I was in a damnable state of nerves. You did some pretty drastic things to me, Jane, and when I left the ship I was as near to a breakdown as I've ever been in my life. I realized the truth of what my doctors had been telling me: I'd no emotional reserves to draw on and would collapse in a crisis. Well, *you* were the crisis and I *did* collapse. I lived on the island for three weeks, and in all that time I never saw a newspaper, never listened to a radio and was completely incommunicado with the paper. By the time I returned to England the Waterman affair was dead. Damn it, Jane, you know there's nothing more dead than yesterday's news, and that's how it was with Colin.'

'Didn't Frank Preston tell you anything?'

'Why would he talk about you? Particularly since I'd cabled to him the morning I left the ship to give you six months' salary.'

'I see. And of course he assumed you were so annoyed about my masquerading as the Belton heiress that you never wanted to talk about me again.'

He nodded, the pressure of his hands relaxing but his fingers still warm on her skin.

Though she longed to believe him, there was something else she had to know. 'Didn't Claire say anything to you? I know you've been seeing her a great deal.'

'I've been seeing a lot of women a great deal,' he said roughly. 'But none of it helped. They only made it worse because I kept comparing them with you.' The pressure of his hands was heavier again. 'Claire never said a word about Colin and I didn't see any reason to mention him either.'

'You know why she didn't tell you, don't you?'

For the first time humour lightened his face. 'At the risk

of appearing conceited I must confess that I do. She knew it would take very little for me to come running after you. My God, Jane, you don't know how near I've been to doing it. Even if Janey hadn't told me the truth I'd have come to find you. In fact, I'd already asked Preston for your address.'

She longed to believe him, yet found it difficult, and seeing her doubt, he sighed. 'Ask Janey. When she came into my office I'd just scribbled your address down on my pad. In fact the first thing I asked her when she came in was where I could find you that day.'

He pulled her closer, her pink chiffon skirts brushing against his leg. 'We've wasted so much time, don't let's waste any more. There's a lot we've got to talk about, but it can wait until later. Now there's only one thing I want to do, and that's hold you in my arms like this' – his body was warm against hers – 'and kiss you like this.' His mouth touched her own, their breath mingling. 'The last time I held you in my arms I behaved like —'

'Don't let's talk about that either!'

She put her arms round his neck and caressed his hair and the side of his face. Their kiss was long and deep but tender – the kiss a man gives to the woman who means the ultimate in his life, whom he wants to share not only his passion but his love.

She was the first to draw back, smoothing her hair, wiping away a tear.

'How will you like being Mrs Stephen Drake?' he asked her huskily. 'I won't let you go on working, Jane. I want to look after you and protect you.'

'And I want to look after you,' she said, and knew a longing to give him all the love and understanding he lacked.

Stephen caught her hand and raised it to his lips, then close together they walked across the lawn towards the house, stopping behind a flowering shrub that hid them from the crowded terrace.

'This is going to be for ever, Jane,' he said quietly. 'From now on your work is going to be me.'

'From now on my *life* is going to be you,' she corrected, and felt his arms come around her again, his face blotting out the sky and the sun.

'Oh, Stephen,' she said, and as his lips came down on hers she was enveloped in a happiness that could never be penetrated, never be dissolved.

Why the smile?

... because she has just received her **Free Harlequin Romance Catalogue!**

... and now she has a complete listing of the many, many Harlequin Romances still available.

... and now she can pick out titles by her favorite authors or fill in missing numbers for her library.

You too may have a **Free Harlequin Romance Catalogue** (and a smile!), simply by mailing in the coupon below.